Sol A

D1520831

THE NEIGHBOR

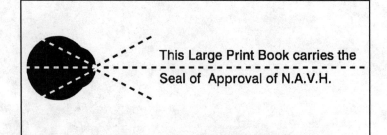

This Large Print Book carries the
Seal of Approval of N.A.V.H.

TEXAS NEIGHBORS, BOOK 2

THE NEIGHBOR

GRACE FOR NEW BEGINNINGS ABIDES IN THIS ENDEARING ROMANCE

DEBRA WHITE SMITH

THORNDIKE PRESS
A part of Gale, Cengage Learning

GALE
CENGAGE Learning™

Detroit • New York • San Francisco • New Haven, Conn • Waterville, Maine • London

GALE
CENGAGE Learning

Thorndike Press, a part of Gale, Cengage Learning.

 LIBRARY OF CONGRESS CATALOGING-IN-PUBLICATION DATA

Smith, Debra White.
    The neighbor : grace for new beginnings abides in this endearing romance / by Debra White Smith.
        p. cm. — (Texas neighbors ; bk. 2) (Thorndike Press large print Christian fiction)
        Originally appeared in the anthology Texas neighbors.
Uhrichsville, Ohio : Barbour Pub., 1998.
        ISBN-13: 978-1-4104-1013-9 (alk. paper)
        ISBN-10: 1-4104-1013-7 (alk. paper)
        1. Texas—Fiction. 2. Large type books. I. Smith, Debra White. Texas neighbors. II. Title.
PS3569.M5178N45 2008
813'.54—dc22   2008029340

Published in 2008 by arrangement with Barbour Publishing, Inc.

Printed in the United States of America
1 2 3 4 5 6 7 12 11 10 09 08

THE NEIGHBOR

CHAPTER 1

"I knew you shouldn't have taken two weeks off work. You're so bored, you're already spying on the neighbors!"

Dr. Alissa Carrington jumped, her heart skipping a beat. She turned to face her best friend and dental office partner, Dr. Trena Selver. "Don't ever sneak up on me like that again! I almost had a heart attack!" Alissa carefully stepped down from the patio chair she'd been standing on to see over the cedar privacy fence.

"So, what's so interesting next door?" Trena asked. Without waiting for an answer, she climbed onto the chair and peered over the fence. "Ah ha! Now I know why you wanted to stay home instead of hitting the beach. He's gorgeous."

"Get down from there!" Alissa hissed as Trena dimpled into a flirtatious smile and waved. Grabbing Trena's hand, Alissa yanked her from the chair. "You've got this all wrong! I wasn't watching *him*. Police have been crawling all over that place since this morning. They're investigating the —"

"So you've started spying." Trena raised her dark brows. "FBI agent — forget this dentistry stuff."

Alissa, lifting her shoulder-length hair off her perspiring neck, inhaled the scent of her suntan lotion. "If you'd just listen . . ."

"Hello there, Frito," Trena said, bending over to pet Alissa's large gray mutt as he scurried under the fence via his recently dug hole.

Alissa rolled her eyes. It looked to her like Trena was the one who was bored. And when she got bored, it seemed she couldn't stay on the same subject more than two seconds.

"Would you listen to me?" Alissa insisted. "The guy next door is putting in a pool, and they dug up some human bones."

"What?" Trena's eyes widened, as if she'd seen a ghost.

"I said human bones. Dead people. Probably murdered!"

"And I thought you'd have nothing to do if you didn't go to the beach with me, but it looks like you've got plenty here to keep you occupied. With this kind of excitement, you could spy for a whole decade!"

"Very funny." Crossing her arm, Alissa watched Frito trot to the far corner of the freshly mowed lawn, and she wondered what she'd have to do to keep the mutt in his own territory. So far, he'd dug three holes to "escape" next door. He was obviously restless in his own yard, a yard Alissa meticulously cared for. Red geraniums, yellow roses, and tender dogwood saplings adorned the landscape, while potted ferns decorated her huge patio and the nearby glassed-in sunroom.

"Well, I'm leaving for the beach this afternoon," Trena said, dismissing Alissa's news for her own. "That's what I came to tell you. Cameron found out last night he could have this week off after all. So he, his parents, and I are heading out for Corpus Christi in about thirty minutes." She checked her watch, and then frowned at Alissa. "I was going to try to talk you into going, but I can see you're too enthralled with what's-his-face next door."

"Not with *him*. I was just curious about the bones."

"Right. Whatever you say." Trena rolled her eyes then frowned again. "But you need to be careful. The bones business is creepy!"

"It's not like it involves me or anything! Why are you always so paranoid?"

"I'm not. I'm just cautious. Well, gotta go," Trena said dismissing the topic as she was so apt to do. With a quick hug, she was off to spend the week with her fiancé.

Alissa stared at the fence. Should she go introduce herself to her new neighbor and apologize for her own spying and Trena's freshness? Trena always had been a flirt while Alissa was the serious one. Even in high school, Trena had been the cheerleader, Alissa, the valedictorian.

She stared up at the row of six evenly spaced windows that lined the back of her vintage 1920, two-story frame house. She should be repapering her bedroom, not worrying about what was going on next door. Hadn't the remodeling been her sole goal for this vacation?

Maybe she *was* bored. Perhaps her curiosity about the discovery next door had served the same purpose as lying in the east Texas sun the last two days. Procrastination. She was putting off the papering, basically because she'd rather be outside in her yard than stuck in the house.

She reflected for a moment longer, then brightened. The sun was shining! The red birds were chirping! And she was on vacation! With an impish smirk, which completely dismissed the wallpaper, Alissa grabbed her red swimsuit cover and wrapped it around her slender waist. The remodeling could wait. What was happening next door was far more interesting.

Barefooted, she picked her way over the cool stepping-stones that dotted the path to her rickety backyard gate, a gate that needed a fresh coat of white paint. Perhaps she'd paint the gate before papering her room. At least it would be an outside job. Accompanied by the protest of squeaking hinges, Alissa stepped through the gate, circled to the right, and stood peering into her neighbor's backyard.

He was bent over a mound of freshly dug earth, talking intently to the policewoman. A policewoman who seemed more interested in him than in the investigation. Trena had been right on one count — he was gorgeous.

Straight blond, sun-streaked hair touched the collar of his teal shirt in a casual yet attractive style. He needed a shave. And he wasn't much taller than Alissa. About five-eleven. Probably early thirties. Just Alissa's type. The type who looked like he'd be at home on a football field but would rather read or discuss horticulture while lounging around the pool in cutoffs. The type that made Alissa want to reach for her binoculars.

But was he a Christian? Dating a non-Christian had already gotten her into trouble once. For the moment Alissa pushed aside the thought. She didn't want to recall the painful memories, which often haunted her, especially not just before meeting someone new.

"Excuse me," Alissa said, nervously clearing her throat. He glanced up, stared at her blankly, and then smiled to reveal a row of white teeth. Alissa's throat went dry. That smile would probably stop traffic in downtown Dallas.

"Hi. Did you decide to come get a closer look?" he said in a soft, East Coast dialect.

So he'd seen her watching, just as she'd suspected. Alissa hoped her warming cheeks weren't as red as they felt. "Sorry about that. But . . . neighbors don't dig up human bones every day. And, um —"

"I'd probably have spied on you, too." His teasing gray eyes suggested a double meaning.

"My grandmother has always said my curiosity was going to get me killed."

"Let's hope not," he said, walking toward her.

As he neared, Alissa realized his excess

stubble was actually the beginnings of a new beard.

"Here, let me get the gate." He reached for the metal latch.

"That's not necessary. I just wanted to introduce myself and apologize for being so nosy."

"It's quite all right. I don't blame you, really. The last thing I ever expected to do was find human bones in my backyard. This is really weird."

"I know. Makes you wonder about your house's former owner, doesn't it?" Alissa glanced at his sprawling red brick house.

"Yeah. Did you know him?"

"Just barely. I'd only been here two months when he sold to you."

"Ever notice anything strange?"

"No. But I stay so busy with my practice — I'm a dentist. Anyway, work keeps me busy, and I don't get to socialize much."

"Are Tuesdays your days off then?"

"No. I'm on vacation. My partner just left for the beach." Alissa broke eye contact, her cheeks warming again. "She's the one who waved to you."

The policewoman discreetly cleared her throat.

"Well, I guess I need to get back home. Oh, by the way," Alissa added as an afterthought, "I'm really sorry about my dog getting into your backyard. I guess I'm going to have to start keeping him indoors."

"It's okay. Really. He plays with Samantha."

"Samantha? So you have a family?" Disappointment stabbed Alissa. She thought he might have winced, but his next words banished that suspicion.

"Yeah." He shrugged his muscular shoulders and grinned. "I guess, if you can call a cat 'family.' "

Smiling, Alissa tried to hide her relief. "Frito always has been partial to cats. I think his mother must have been one."

Chuckling, he glanced over his shoulder toward the policewoman.

"Well, I — I guess I'll get back to my sunbathing. Let me know if I can help," Alissa said.

"Can you cook?"

She blinked. "Excuse me?"

"You said to let you know if you could help. It would really *help* me to have lunch with you." With a quirk of his left brow, his near-black eyes took on a teasing gleam. "That is, if you can cook."

"I can't. I'm a lousy cook." Alissa, her heart warming, dimpled into what she hoped was her most attractive smile. "But

14

I'm the fastest dialer in Tyler, Texas. I could call for a pizza."

"Sounds good. Give me about an hour. I think it's good to get to know your neighbors. I'm Brad, by the way. Brad Ratner."

"Nice to meet you, Brad. I'm Alissa Carrington."

CHAPTER 2

An hour later, Alissa set the aromatic pizza on her antique dining table. She'd spent the last hour showering and trying to do something with her hair and makeup. Not that there was much she could do. It amazed her that she could completely rearrange somebody's teeth but couldn't get much more than a bronze lipstick on right. And her blond hair never did anything but hang straight. So what was the use?

Thankful for her naturally rosy cheeks and brown eyes and brows, Alissa made sure the back of her red T-shirt was tucked into her denim skirt. Then, with a flick of her fingers, she popped open the pizza box. If Brad didn't like pepperoni, she was in trouble. But Sherman had always liked it.

Alissa's hands stilled. Sherman. The very thought she'd fought to suppress. The same swordlike guilt, which always accompanied his name, seemed to pierce her soul.

16

"Why are you doing this to me?" he demanded. "How could you? Don't you know I love you? I thought you loved me!"

Alissa closed her eyes as the guilt blew through her being like tattering winds. "I'm sorry," she whispered to no one and wondered if she'd ever be able to forgive herself.

Sherman Devereauz, formerly one of Tyler's most prominent surgeons, had "conveniently" transferred his practice to Dallas immediately after Alissa had broken off their engagement eight months ago. To this day, Alissa wished she'd used more wisdom in her relationship with him. From the start she'd known he was an agnostic, at best. But his dark good looks and easy charm, along with her loneliness, had persuaded her that perhaps she could "change" him. As the wedding date neared, though, Alissa realized he wasn't going to change, that all her attempts to introduce him to Christ were in vain. She then envisioned herself taking her future children to church by herself, a trap she'd always wished to avoid. So she'd ended the engagement and vowed never to make the same mistake again.

The ringing phone broke into her reflections. Biting her thumbnail in anxiety, Alissa debated whether to take the call or to allow her answering machine to record a message. Her eighty-year-old grandmother hadn't yet placed her daily call, and Alissa feared this was it. Her phone conversations always lasted thirty minutes at the very least — thirty minutes Alissa couldn't spare just now.

Loyalty, however, forced her to pick up the cordless phone on the fourth ring. Her suspicions were well founded. "Alissa, are you going to take me to the church social tonight?" her grandmother asked before Alissa could say hello. "You know I don't want to miss it. Lila Dally is going, and she's taking that sweet potato casserole I gave her the recipe for. You know, the one with the pineapple in it? Anyway, she tells everybody it's *her* recipe. I just can't stand it anymore. I just can't! I'm gonna make those sweet potatoes and tell everybody it's *my* recipe. That ought to fix her up right and good. And another thing —"

The doorbell rang. "Grandma, I've got to go. But I'll pick you up at six thirty like we planned."

"That Reynolds man has gone too far this time. Do you know he actually asked me to go to the museum with him? And him an eighty-year-old man. Why, if he thinks I'm gonna start dating at this age, well . . ."

The doorbell rang again. "Grandma, there's someone at the door. I'll call you back." Alissa stared in consternation through the kitchen and toward the massive oak door.

"... that Samuel Reynolds can just find himself another woman. I tell you —"

"Grandma, there's a *man* at my door. I've got a *lunch date.*" Alissa knew that would do the trick. She also knew she'd pay for it later. Her grandmother would want every detail.

"A man! Well, why didn't you say so? You're already thirty years old, and it's high time you got another regular man friend. Wait till I tell your father. He'll be tickled down to his toes. Okay." The phone clicked.

With an indulgent grin, Alissa hung up. She'd never known her grandmother to say "good-bye." It was always "okay." Alissa rushed across her living room's rose-colored carpet toward the door, reaching it in the middle of Brad's third ring.

"I was beginning to wonder if I'd hallucinated our conversation," he said with a lopsided grin. Alissa, trying not to appear too eager, smiled. Faded blue jeans and a crisp white cotton shirt had never looked better. Add to that the hint of mystery his new beard gave to his smoky eyes, and the casual yet classy combination was almost too compelling.

Bells of caution sounded through Alissa's mind. *Don't get too attracted until you know more!* "Sorry 'bout that. I was on the phone with my grandmother — my father's mother. I think the house could be burning down around me and she'd just keep right on talking. Come on in."

Chuckling, Brad passed her, leaving a sporty citrus scent in his wake. "She's probably crazy about you."

"Yeah. I guess I am about her, too. My mother died when I was fifteen. Grandma was widowed shortly after that. Grandma and Father finished raising me together." *And God only knows how much I still miss my mother.*

"It's nice to have a family," Brad said, a dark shadow flitting across his eyes. But the shadow left just as quickly as he handed her a bottle of cold soda. "I thought I'd supply the drinks."

"Thanks. Kitchen's this way." Having dated some of the tall, dark, handsome types, Alissa decided then and there that this guy made most of the dark handsomes she knew look like something Frito would drag up. Not that Brad was perfect. His brows were too heavy and his nose a bit too long for model perfection, but his physique made up for those flaws. *He must work out regularly,* she thought. His shoulders were too broad, his waist too narrow for any other explanation.

"Nice house," Brad said. Alissa glanced behind her and took a split second to admire the classic Queen Anne look she'd managed to accomplish in the last two months. "Thanks. I've had some work done on it. New carpet, new paint, new kitchen cabinets. And I'm supposed to be finishing my upstairs bedroom — wallpaper and maybe paint — but haven't had the motivation to start."

"It's this east Texas heat and humidity. It'll turn you into a regular lotus-eater."

"Yeah. You'd think being raised here, I'd be used to it. But July and August do this to me every year." Alissa opened the cabinet and grabbed two paper plates. "I'll serve you on my finest china."

"Good. I hate doing dishes. Mind if I get the ice in the glasses?"

"No, not at all. There's a full ice bucket in the freezer. Glasses are over there." Alissa pointed to the new oak cabinet beside her stainless steel sink. "So what did you find out about the cemetery in your backyard?"

"You've got that right. It is like a cem-

21

etery." The ice crackled as he plopped the cubes into tall glasses. "The best we can tell, there are two bodies over there. And the guy from the forensics lab says it looks like they've been there awhile. They won't know for a couple of months, though, exactly how long."

"That kinda gives me the creeps." Chills raced along Alissa's spine.

"Me, too."

"So are they going to question Mr. . . . what was the man's name who lived there before you?"

"Jenkins. Yeah. They're supposed to call him in today."

"Do you think he's responsible?"

"I don't know. He seemed nice enough when we closed the house deal." Brad set the glasses full of ice on the table, and Alissa poured the fizzing soda. "But then, that doesn't really mean anything."

"Yeah. Looks can be deceiving," Alissa said.

"The investigating officer is going to question our other neighbors. Maybe they'll know something. Man, the police and investigators have been crawling all over the place. Right now, there's not anyone over there. . . . But they'll be back."

"I guess this means your pool project's on

hold then."

"Yeah. I'll just have to keep going to the YMCA for a while. I have to swim regularly — doctors orders."

"Oh?"

"I was involved in an — an accident two years ago." Brad, sitting down, made a big job of placing two pieces of pizza on his plate.

Alissa wondered if he was trying to hide something. He'd seemed comfortable when he first arrived. But the longer he stayed, the less comfortable he seemed, and the more tense his mouth became.

"Anyway, I've got a hip injury. And the swimming helps it." Brad's clipped words closed the subject and left Alissa wondering what had happened.

She took the seat across from him and helped herself to a piece of the steaming pizza. "I hope you like pepperoni."

"It's my favorite."

"Really? Mine, too."

"And they have something in common!" Brad said over a mouthful.

With a smile, Alissa bit into the spicy pizza. She hoped they had one other thing in common. "So, what do you do for a living?"

"I'm an — an artist. I work mostly in oils."

"An artist? Really? I've always admired people who can paint. I can hardly draw a stick man."

"I've always admired people who have the patience to go into the medical field. How'd you decide to become a dentist?"

"I guess my grandmother had something to do with it. She always encouraged me to make a career for myself. And when I had to have braces at twelve and realized what a difference it made in my looks and the way I felt about myself, I knew I wanted to make other people just as happy as I was. I'll admit there are some things about it I don't like. But overall, it's a great career."

Alissa started to mention her two-week missions trip to Africa last fall but stopped herself. Part of the reason she'd gone into a medical profession was to share her skills with those in need. She didn't feel a full-time call to the mission field, but planned to spend her life participating in mission teams every chance she got.

She couldn't help but notice how skillfully Brad had steered the conversation away from himself. Alissa also noted that he'd glanced at his watch three times in the last five minutes. He was trying very hard to feign politeness, but his readiness to leave was obvious. Oh well, this lunch date had been his idea, and Alissa would probably just chalk it up to a friendly neighborhood encounter anyway.

"It's hard to believe you ever had anything wrong with your teeth," Brad said softly. "You have such a beautiful smile."

Alissa, glancing up from studying her soda, encountered a mixture of agony and admiration stirring in his eyes. Her stomach tightening, she swallowed. This man was sending conflicting signals and managing to thoroughly confuse her.

"Thanks," she squeaked. "I guess beauty is in the eyes of the beholder, because —"

"I think I should leave," Brad said, then stood.

"Oh . . . well, okay." *You're starting to sound like Grandma.*

"Thanks for the pizza," he said, pulling his eelskin billfold from his hip pocket. "Here. That should cover the cost." He laid two bills on the table.

"No. Th–that's okay. I was g–going to order it for myself anyway," Alissa stuttered in confusion.

"I'll let you know what happens with the investigation," he clipped, ignoring her protest. With a swift turn he then rushed out of the house like a pack of demons was after him.

■ ■ ■ ■

Brad shut Alissa's front door, swallowed hard, and took a deep breath. *Well, you just made a one-hundred-percent fool of yourself.* If she just hadn't used Dana's favorite cliché: Beauty is in the eyes of the beholder. But that, coupled with his feelings of guilt, had been all he could handle. So he'd run. With shaking fingers, Brad rubbed the nape of his neck and slowly walked back toward his house.

He'd invited himself for lunch before he knew what he was doing. Brad couldn't remember being so befuddled by a woman since . . . "Since Dana," he whispered. And he wasn't ready to be involved with someone else. It seemed disloyal to Dana, disloyal to Kara.

A mistake. That's what lunch with Alissa Carrington had been. A huge mistake. And he'd never have made the date if she hadn't been so attractive. But there she'd stood in a red swimsuit wrap, no makeup, looking as hot and sweaty as he felt. Yet still she was a knockout, with hair the color of honey, eyes like brown velvet, a cute little pug nose, and a full-lipped smile that revealed a row of near-perfect teeth. Regardless of her looks, though, he couldn't even think of developing more than a passing acquaintance. He simply couldn't be disloyal to Dana.

Walking to his backyard gate, Brad stepped through it and scoffed at himself. He'd told her he was an artist. What kind of an artist went two years without picking up a brush? Brad had barely touched the fortune his talent had amassed. He had enough old paintings to keep the galleries happy for another year, but he wasn't producing anything new. What would happen when he ran out of the old stuff?

Samantha's meowed greeting from near the fence helped Brad push aside the disturbing thought. "Hey, Sam. Come here and I'll scratch your ears." Picking up the yellow-striped cat, he walked toward the huge hole in his backyard. Maybe the upheaval over these bodies would jar him back into his creative mode.

Then he saw it. Just a slight movement from the corner of his eyes, the kind of movement a quick glance might explain as harmless. But this time the movement wasn't harmless.

"Hey, you!" Brad yelled as a shadowed figure rushed from his massive patio window and through his house.

27

CHAPTER 3

Alissa stepped out of her front door and walked toward her Mustang convertible sitting in the circular driveway. Brad had been gone exactly five minutes. Five minutes! And Alissa now needed a fifty-minute drive that she hoped would help blow thoughts of him from her mind.

Her common sense told her to forget she'd ever met him. But something in her spirit seemed compellingly drawn to him. This feeling was different from any she'd ever experienced, different even from her initial attraction to Sherman. This was something akin to . . . perhaps it was compassion.

Sighing, Alissa walked across her landscaped front yard and told herself that the man was none of her concern. Yet, something about his pleading gray eyes haunted her soul, tore at her heart.

With another sigh, she fumbled for her

keys in the bottom of her oversized leather purse. "Chalk it up to experience, Alissa ol' girl," she mumbled with a smirk. "Never have lunch with men with bones in their backyard."

The words had no sooner left her lips than a hard shove in the center of her back sent her sprawling to the sidewalk, her purse flying through the air. Her knees and palms felt as if they'd been doused in acid. She yelped with pain.

A dark-clad, masked person raced past her without so much as a backward glance.

"Are you okay?" a breathless man asked. Brad, bent over her, his eyes dark with concern. Had he been trying to protect her? Or was this just wishful thinking, hopeful longing?

Alissa, standing up, tried to regain her equilibrium and make sense of the last few harried seconds. "I think I'm all right. Guess I just skinned my knees and hands. Who was that? What's going on?" She turned to see the dark figure round the street corner two blocks away.

"I'll be back," Brad mumbled, before streaking away after the mysterious stranger. Yet Brad wasn't fast enough; the sound of a cranking engine and squealing wheels filled the air just as he reached the block's end.

Minutes later, he stood beside Alissa. "That person was just in my house," he huffed, his eyes churning.

She gasped. "Did he take anything?"

"I don't think so. It didn't look like he was carrying anything. But I didn't take time to look in the house. I just started the chase."

"Did you see the car?" Alissa glanced up the peaceful street in search of movement. But the only movement along the rows of emerald yards was a water sprinkler three doors down.

"No. Are you sure you're all right?" With a wince, she pulled aside her sarong skirt and examined her throbbing knees, now bloodied. Glad her thong sandals required no hose, she gingerly touched the red skin around the scrapes. "I think I'll live. It doesn't look any worse than the falls I took off my bike as a kid. I'll mend." Another wince, and she examined the heels of her aching palms.

Brad, however, didn't seem quite as optimistic. "Come on," he said, grabbing her arm. "I'm going to bandage your knees."

"No, really! I'm okay!" Alissa protested as he propelled her to his house.

"Don't argue. It's no use. If your knees get infected, I'll never forgive myself."

"You need to worry about calling the police. I can bandage my own knees. I'm a doctor, remember? Your having to do it is ridiculous." *But not half as ridiculous as the way you acted over lunch.* Alissa didn't know whether to be glad for his concern or aggravated at his vacillating behavior.

His lips tight, Brad opened his beige front door and led Alissa into the spacious living room. *"Now sit!"* he commanded, nudging her toward a white leather chair.

She lowered herself into the chair's soft folds. "Okay. But call the police before you help me. And don't touch anything. Maybe they can find some fingerprints." She smiled to herself. Maybe all those old Dick Tracy movies would pay off after all.

Nodding, Brad turned toward the ivory phone sitting on a nearby brass and glass table. Alissa glanced around the room. Except for a thin layer of dust on the tables, the house smelled clean, looked clean. And it seemed to be an extension of his personality. Understated class. The fine balance of creams and whites gave the rooms an airy quality the vintage 1950 house lacked on it's own. Even the rows of ocean paintings lining the walls perfectly complemented the room's light décor.

She stood to get a closer view of the paint-

31

ings. Each had its own personality. Each depicted the sea in a particular mood of upheaval or calm. And each held the same mesmerizing, illusive quality . . . the same sort of thing that stirred in the depths of Brad's eyes. They had to be his work.

So intent was she on examining the paintings that she didn't see the petite glass lamp table until she stumbled into it. With a quick downward glance, she steadied the porcelain oriental lamp before it could topple to its death. Then something else on the table snared her attention. A Bible. A worn Bible. But, it, too, was covered in a film of dust and had the name "Brad Ratner" printed in gold against navy leather. The presence of the Bible, once well used but now neglected, spoke volumes. And Alissa momentarily mused over the meaning, a meaning that added to Brad's mysterious appeal.

"Sit!" he commanded, hanging up the phone. "You can't escape. You might as well stop trying."

"I'm not trying to escape. I wanted to look at your paintings," Alissa snapped, his domineering attitude starting to annoy her.

"After the bandages." A coaxing, knowing smile tilted his lips as if he knew he'd gone too far with the commands.

Despite herself, Alissa returned his smile

and resumed her place in the chair. The man could probably charm the stripes off a tiger. "What did the police say?" Alissa asked, hoping to hide the effect he had on her.

"The investigators are already on their way back. The office is going to radio them about what happened." He disappeared down the hall to return minutes later, carrying antiseptic gauze bandages and tape.

"You need to be warned. I'm a terrible patient. And if you put anything on my knees to make them burn worse than they're already burning, I'll scream."

Brad broke into an indulgent smile. "This is hydrogen peroxide. It shouldn't burn, little girl." Dropping to his knees, he began swabbing her wounds.

Had he just been flirting with her? Alissa wanted to shake her head to clear the confusion. One minute, he rushed from her house as if she was repulsive. And the next, he was flirting with her.

Regardless of Brad's strange behavior and her speculations about his faith, something bizarre had taken place in his backyard, a fact that Alissa couldn't ignore. Her curiosity began to whirl with unanswered questions. "Do you think that person in your house had anything to do with the bones in your backyard?" she asked, admiring the swift gentleness of his long, artist's fingers.

"Could be. But how? I mean, nobody knows I found the bones but you and me and the police."

"True. But I was curious enough to . . . to eavesdrop. Maybe one of the other neighbors did the same. Think about it. You have five candidates. There's me. There's the person on the other side of your house. Then there's the three people whose property borders your backyard fence but whose houses face the next street over. Any one of them could know that the bones were unearthed and that there was a lull in the police investigation."

"Good thinking. So would that mean one of the neighbors could be the murderer, not Mr. Jenkins?"

"Maybe."

"But what reason would he have for breaking into my house? The person could have just used the fence gate. But wait a minute!"

Brad looked up from Alissa's knees. "I came through the gate. Maybe the person entered that way but had to exit through my house so I wouldn't see him."

"Was your patio door unlocked?" Alissa glanced toward the door to see if there were signs of forced entry.

"Probably, I'm not the world's best at locking my doors. Besides, I was just going to be next door with you. I didn't think anything would happen."

"Do you think there might be something at the grave site that could incriminate someone?"

"Could be. I guess we could go look around before the police arrive." Brad placed the final piece of tape on her bandaged knees, and then took her hands in his to swab the scrapes with the cool peroxide.

Alissa, trying to deny the tingles working their way up her arms, finally decided it was no use. She reacted to Brad Ratner like dynamite with a short fuse.

"There. You should feel better now," Brad said seconds later. Seeming to carefully avoid eye contact, he stood and gathered the first-aid supplies.

"Thanks, I do." Then Alissa searched for something, anything to say. The awkward silence settling between them like a fog of unanswered questions didn't help her search.

"I'm sorry about the way I acted over lunch," he finally blurted to the gauze bandages.

"Oh, well, it's okay . . ." Alissa trailed off

uncertainly.

"No, it isn't. I — I acted like a fool." Brad set the first-aid supplies on a nearby table and walked across the room to look out the patio window.

Speechless, Alissa stared at his back. She recognized the turmoil churning in him. It didn't take a world-famous psychiatrist to see that something dark and dreadful haunted this man's dreams, his every waking hour. Pain. She'd seen it in his eyes and identified with it.

Perhaps that was part of the attraction. A shared emotion. Hadn't she known the pain when cancer wasted her vivacious mother into a bony shadow? Didn't she have an occasional cry for what could have been? For how proud Harriet Carrington would have been that her daughter was now a successful dentist?

"I've got a very good explanation for the way I acted," Brad said tightly. Then, turning to face her, he ran his hand through his hair where it touched his collar. "But . . . but I — I can't tell you . . ." His voice trailed off.

"It's okay," Alissa said. Standing, she walked across the room to place her hand on his taut forearm. Covering her hand with his, Brad looked directly into her eyes.

"You're a beautiful woman, Alissa Carrington. And I know we could be really good together — as friends. Would you be my friend? I can't offer anything else. But I need a friend right now."

Swallowing, Alissa nodded, and her heart palpitated with a mixture of disappointment and relief. So all he wanted was friendship. As far as she was concerned, he was the most attractive man she'd ever met. A combination of ruggedness and gentleness, of past hurts and hints of future happiness. Mere friendship. This had to be poetic justice. Isn't that what she'd told Sherman?

Sherman. The very thought of him, and her chest tightened. She'd devastated the man, had never seen a person so stricken as he was the night she broke off their engagement. Her honest explanation hadn't helped, had only made him angrier. "You're throwing me over for God," he'd yelled in bitter accusation.

If Brad didn't share her faith, though, his request for mere friendship was for the best. But then there was his personalized Bible, which showed signs of past diligent use.

In confusion, Alissa turned to open the patio door. "Let's go look at the grave site and forget lunch ever happened. We'll just start from here," she squeaked out with forced cheerfulness.

I should have known she'd do this, the invader thought. Lips twisted, hair disheveled, she stared at herself in the teak dresser's mirror. On the queen-sized bed lay the black pants, shirt, and ski mask she'd just removed.

Louanne thinks she's so smart. Just because that nosy Brad Ratner dug up her grave and she escaped, she thinks she can just come back into the neighborhood like nothing ever happened — like I never even killed her. Henry says she calls herself Alissa Carrington. But that's a lie. Nobody has that golden hair and wide-eyed innocent look but Louanne Young. And she must die again!

CHAPTER 4

Alissa peered into the shallow hole in Brad's backyard. Even in the summer heat, the thought of the wicked deed that had taken place here made her shiver. The smell of freshly dug soil, the reality of murder, and the hint of future danger cloaked the scene in a disturbing aura.

"And that's all I know," Brad told the television investigator. He had related the events that led up to his discovery of the bones.

Shortly after the police arrived, the television crew had surfaced, equipped with their "breaking story" curiosity and what seemed a million questions.

As the camerawoman scanned the yard landscaped in evergreens and ornamental shrubs, Alissa compulsively tried to step out of the camera's pathway, only to bump into an investigation police officer.

"Excuse me," she mumbled. She glanced

up to see the camera aimed smack at her. *Oh, great!* Alyssa thought. *One more thing to explain to my grandmother.* After Emily Carrington viewed the evening news, she wouldn't be happy until Alissa brought her to Brad's backyard for her own inspection. Alissa wasn't the only one in the family with ample curiosity.

While yet another investigator cornered Brad, Alissa decided to take her leave. She'd fruitlessly answered a few questions about the person who knocked her down. When the police and camera crew realized how little she knew, they converged on Brad. Now she was simply in the way, a mere observer.

That was how she felt in relation to Brad, too. Their new "friendship" was obviously going to be characterized by Brad holding her at arm's length. He'd hardly glanced at her since the investigators arrived.

With a sigh, Alissa turned toward the gate, only to glimpse a flash of white from behind the cedar fence spanning the back of Brad's yard. Then the sounds of metal against wood, and a resounding feminine howl, pierced the neighborhood's tranquility. Every gaze instinctively turned towards Brad's fence as low moans issued from the other sides.

40

"I'll see if she needs help," Alissa said, rushing from the yard. She quickly rounded the block and entered the woman's backyard, where she found her propped against the fence, gingerly rubbing her right ankle.

She wore an oversized red housedress that Alissa figured was an attempt to conceal her plumpish curves. Her bleached-blond hair was bound in a white cotton scarf, a scarf that hadn't stopped one of the pink sponge rollers from dislodging; it dangled between her eyes by a wisp of kinky, pale hair. Her lips, meticulously painted a neon orange, grimaced at the obvious pain ravaging her ankle.

"Are you okay?" Kneeling beside the six-tyish woman who smelled of lavender soap, Alissa noted the flimsy aluminum ladder lying in a twisted heap beside a row of climbing red roses.

"I think I'm fine. I was just — just tryin' to cut some roses when the ladder gave way and I fell and twisted my ankle," the woman whined in a heavy east Texas drawl.

Yeah, and I'm Peter Pan, Alissa thought. Nobody cut roses without shears, which were conspicuously absent. Alissa figured the woman had been spying, just as she herself had spied earlier. Biting her lips, Alissa stopped her judgmental thoughts.

41

After all, she'd been no less nosy herself.

She bent to examine an ankle that showed no signs of injury. "Would you like me to drive you to a clinic? A quick X-ray will tell you if it's broken or just sprained."

"No, no, that's okay, darlin'. I don't think it's broken. All I need to do is maybe put it up on a chair."

"Elizabeth? Are you all right?" a raspy voice called from the white brick house's back door. Turning, Alissa encountered a woman as thin as Elizabeth was plump. Scrawny described her best. A dried-up scrawny prune with unkempt Lucille Ball red hair, and a crooked, wart-encrusted nose like the Wicked Witch of the West. Her deeply winkled brow creasing, she raced toward her friend.

"I was in my front yard when I heard you yell. But you sounded like you were inside. I knocked and knocked. When I didn't get any answer, I got worried and used the hidden key. What happened?" she gushed.

A flush crept up Elizabeth's neck to stain her smooth colorless cheeks. "I — I was cutting some roses and fell."

"Cutting some roses! I thought you left that to the yardman. What's gotten into you?"

As the newcomer bent over her friend's

42

ankle, Alissa stepped back.

"Well . . ." Elizabeth seemed at a loss for an answer.

"I guess I'll go now," Alissa said, purposefully relieving Elizabeth from further embarrassment over her lie.

"Oh, um, thanks for coming over," Elizabeth said. "I'm Elizabeth, by the way, Mrs. Elizabeth Teasedale."

"Nice to meet you, Mrs. Teasedale. I'm Alissa Carrington. I'm the new owner of Mrs. Docker's old house."

"Yeah, we know," the newcomer stated.

"Sadie," Elizabeth gasped.

Sadie stilled as if suddenly realizing what she'd revealed. How did these two women know Alissa when she'd never even met them?

"Oh, I — I mean, nice to meet you," Sadie stuttered, her raspy smoker's voice seeming to scratch every stilted word. "I'm Sadie Horton. My husband, Henry, and I live there." She pointed toward the sprawling, pillared mansion whose emerald-green yard ran to the block's end. Then, with a decisive turn toward Elizabeth, she hiked up her ragged, baggy jeans.

Alissa blinked at the incongruity. How did such a classless, brassy woman come to live in such an elegant home?

43

"Now you're going to the doctor, Lizzy. And no arguments," Sadie said.

Elizabeth, nodding mutely, offered no resistance to her friend's order.

"I really think that's the best idea," Alissa said.

"Thanks again, Dr. Carrington," Elizabeth said.

Figuring that was her cue to leave, Alissa wondered how Elizabeth knew she was a doctor. At the same time, she wondered if there was anything about her that the ladies didn't know.

"Everything okay over here?" a familiar masculine voice asked from the other side of the fence. Nodding, Alissa glanced up to see Brad peering over the cedar boards. She decided to inquire later about the slight slurring of his *r*'s. It suggested perhaps an East Coast influence and, like the man, spoke of culture mixed with down-to-earth casualness.

"Mrs. Teasdale fell from her ladder and hurt her ankle, and Mrs. Horton's going to take her for an X-ray." Alissa turned to the older women and made the appropriate introductions, although she fully suspected it was unnecessary — for the ladies anyway. If they knew Alissa, they probably knew Brad.

"Nice to meet you." Brad, producing his traffic-stopping smile, offered his condolences for Mrs. Teasedale's ankle. Then he lowered his voice to a whisper, and his eyes gleamed with conspiracy. "Oh, and just in case you haven't noticed, I seem to have a little problem in my backyard."

"Oh?" Mrs. Teasedale asked in obviously feigned astonishment.

The woman would starve as an actress, Alissa thought.

"Yes. The pool company dug up some human bones this morning. So don't be shocked if the police come around to ask you a few questions. They're going to be questioning the whole neighborhood, I'm afraid."

No genuine surprise or alarm registered with either woman, and only Sadie replied. "Thanks for the warning," she said, her eyes thin slits of contempt. Apparently she didn't appreciate Brad's humor. Turning her back to Alissa, Sadie began helping her friend to her feet.

"Are you sure you don't want me to help?" Alissa asked, taking a step toward them.

"No," Sadie said, as if to once and for all dismiss Alissa. Raising her brows, Alissa shrugged at Brad, who shrugged in return.

45

■ ■ ■ ■

"The top story this evening involves a bizarre finding which seems to have the makings of a late-night murder mystery," the TV news anchorwoman announced on the five o'clock news.

A smile twisting her lips, the murderer lifted the remote control, started the VCR tape, and increased the television's volume. She listened intently as the investigative reporter related the events, then grinned as the camera panned the yard to reveal Louanne standing beside her grave. Next, a brief interview with that nosy Brad Ratner.

She gritted her teeth. If only he had minded his own business, had never started that pool project, allowing Louanne to escape. Now she would be forced to murder Louanne again.

Reaching for her filterless cigarettes, she laughed and adjusted the VCR to rewatch the story she'd just recorded. It was only a matter of time, mere hours before Louanne would die once more. All she needed to do was crank up the little blue Mustang of hers . . . then whammy! The murderer slammed her right fist against her left palm.

Maybe this time Louanne Young would stay dead.

"Alissa, I saw you on the news tonight. Why didn't you tell me about those bones next door? And that good-lookin' man! Is he the one you had lunch with? Do you think he'd let me see the grave? I can't believe it! Wait till I tell Aubry I saw the grave with my own eyes."

"Grandma, I don't think —" Alissa cradled the cordless phone against her shoulder and tried to brush her hair as her grandmother continued.

"Did you forget you had to pick me up in fifteen minutes for the church social?"

"No. I was headed out the door when you called."

"Okay." With a decisive click the line went dead.

Shaking her head, Alissa turned off the phone, grabbed her keys and purse, put Frito into the backyard, then hurried for the front door. Her earlier speculation about why Mrs. Teasedale and Mrs. Horton knew her identity had died shortly after she'd come home. If they were anything like her grandmother, then they probably knew her shoe size by now.

Alissa hadn't gone back to Brad's after

47

leaving Mrs. Teasedale's yard. She'd come home to paint her backyard gate, and then puttered around in the flowerbeds until nearly time to pick up her grandmother. A quick check of her answering machine had revealed a message from Brad asking her to return his call and an odd message for someone named Louanne. The caller said Louanne was in some sort of trouble.

Smiling slightly, Alissa inserted her key into the locked car door, and then adjusted the hem of her red T-shirt. She ignored the call for Louanne and hadn't had time to call Brad back but planned to when she returned. Of course, they could only be friends, she told herself again. But that didn't stop the tiny spark of hope from igniting within, or the faint, undeniable thrill at the sound of his voice on her answering machine. *Maybe, just maybe,* she thought as she sank into the car seat and placed the key into the ignition. *But are you ready for another relationship? Look what you did to Sherman,* another voice insisted.

Trying to ignore the ever-present guilt, she snapped on her seat belt then fished through her cluttered purse to find her designer sunglasses. It amazed her that she could keep her closets immaculately clean while her purse usually resembled a pack rat's abandoned home. Trena frequently accused her of "repressed slob syndrome," and with a smirk, claimed that it went back to Alissa's childhood.

"Finally," she sighed as she dragged her black sunglasses from the bottom of her purse and put them on. She started to crank the engine, only to stop and adjust the rearview mirror. With everything in place, Alissa turned the ignition key, put the car into drive, drove out of her circular driveway, and began her journey up the hill in front of Brad's house.

Just as she increased her speed, though, a sleek, yellow-striped cat bolted from beside Brad's brick mailbox into the car's path. Alissa, her heart lurching, swerved to the right, and then smashed her foot against the brake pedal, which sank to the floorboard without resistance.

CHAPTER 5

The sounds of glass shattering and metal smashing into brick made Brad drop his ham sandwich in midbite. Only minutes before, he'd seen two children across the street playing catch in the vacant lot. Could one of them have chased the ball into the street and been hit? The little girl wasn't much older than Kara had been. She even had Kara's mahogany curls.

Had it really been two years already? It seemed like yesterday. But the torment, the pain, the misery Brad had experienced was enough to last a lifetime. If only he'd listened to Dana and stayed home that day. If only God hadn't allowed the tragedy.

A lump formed in his throat as his mind flashed images of Kara's limp little body lying dead in his arms, a crimson stain marring her T-shirt. That same fatal morning, she'd said, "Look at my new pink shirt, Daddy!" And he'd promised the T-shirt made her the prettiest little girl in the world. Would he once again cradle a dead little girl in his arms?

The answer lay on the other side of his front door. He hurried to the front door and reached for the brass knob. Brad's hand stopped. Could he face another tragedy? Even someone else's tragedy?

Grinding his teeth, he willed the fear to flee. The paralysis passed. And with a determined twist of the knob he rushed down his porch steps to see Alissa's Mustang enmeshed with what was left of his brick mailbox.

"Alissa!" he croaked. Only seconds before, he'd imagined cradling another dead child. But he'd never thought about the possibility of once again holding, sobbing over, the corpse of a beautiful woman. That possibility vanished, though, as he neared the car and Alissa emerged from behind the wheel.

"I'm — I'm okay," she stammered, a shaking hand covered her heart. "It's just . . . my brakes didn't work. I'm sorry about your mailbox." Tears brimmed her big brown eyes then splashed onto her cheeks one at a time, like fat raindrops taking their precious time to fall.

"Hey, it's all right," he soothed and rushed to her side. Before he knew it Brad had

51

pulled Alissa into his arms for a consoling hug. He'd always said there was nothing more powerful than brown, tear-filled, feminine eyes. Unless, of course, it was the woman in his arms. Or the smell of jasmine perfume. His stomach felt as if he'd jumped from an airplane. And before he could experience any more emotional upheaval, Brad abruptly released her, only to have the jasmine scent linger with him.

Alissa, sniffling twice, produced a tissue from her pocket and wiped her eyes. "I guess I'm crying because I was scared speechless."

"Me, too," he breathed, noticing that the children must have gone back to their homes. "I was afraid someone had hit one of the children who were playing here earlier." Brad swallowed hard against the nausea creeping up his throat. "And then when I saw your car, I was afraid I'd —" He stopped himself short. Brad had almost said "I was afraid I'd lost you." Instead he said, "I was afraid you might have been hurt." He wondered what was going on within himself. Could this attractive dentist be weaving her way into his heart without his consent? His actions and words didn't match his claim of only wanting a friendship.

"Look at my car," Alissa groaned. "My '68 classic is demolished." Samantha yowled innocently from nearby and came to curve her way around Brad's legs. "And it's all because of that cat," Alissa said. "She ran out in front of me. I swerved to miss her, and then couldn't stop. Do you know who she belongs to?"

With an ironic smile, Brad bent to pick up Samantha. "Alissa Carrington, meet Samantha Ratner, my feline companion — and Frito's best friend."

"Oh, no! I just realized . . ." Alissa placed shaking fingers over her rounded lips. "If she hadn't run out in front of me, I probably wouldn't have braked until the next big intersection. Then I could have been . . ." She swallowed as what was left of the color in her cheeks vanished.

"Let's just be thankful you weren't," Brad said with more reassurance than he felt. "When was the last time you had your brakes checked?"

"I had the car serviced just last week. They were supposed to have checked everything. Transmission fluid, oil, brake fluid, and anything else that needs to be checked. I know absolutely nothing about cars."

"Then you know more than I do," Brad mumbled, hating to admit his weakness. His father was a mechanical genius, but that talent somehow skipped Brad, the firstborn, and went to his younger sister, Victoria. "My sister and father are the mechanics in our family. It's rather embarrassing when the college quarterback can't do more than add windshield wiper fluid without creating a total disaster, but his ninety-five pound sister can overhaul her car's carburetor."

Alissa, giving a final dab to the corner of her left eye, giggled. Brad adjusted his thin, black-framed glasses and began to relax for the first time since he'd heard the crash.

"I didn't know you wore glasses," Alissa said absently, her attention still focused on her crumpled car.

"I normally wear contacts," he explained, walking to the car's front bumper. "I'm slightly nearsighted — just enough to be annoying. I'd taken out my contacts earlier, when I went to the Y to swim, and hadn't put them back in." Brad didn't add that all the extra standing around because of the investigation had reactivated an old ache in his right hip. He'd explained to Alissa that he had to swim regularly because of an "accident" — if you could call a bullet wound an accident.

"Excuse me," a timid, high-pitched voice called from behind. "Did you need any help?" Brad turned to see a middle-aged woman of slightly plump build walking toward them. Her mass of short auburn curls framed an oval-shaped face, a face whose best feature was her deep-set, almost turquoise eyes. Whoever she was, she'd been a knockout once. But the beauty of her youth had been diminished by age and the dark circles under her eyes.

"I — I heard the crash," she continued. "I was in my backyard and thought I'd check to see if I needed to call an ambulance."

"Thanks," Alissa said. "But it looks like the only doctor I'm going to need is a car doctor." She waved toward the Mustang's crumpled hood before adding, "My mechanic runs a towing and auto-rebuilding service as part of his business; maybe he can tow the car for me."

The newcomer nodded. "I'm Claire Allen, by the way. Aren't you the dentist who bought Sarah Docker's house?"

Alissa nodded.

"I live right behind you, then."

"Oh, in the cute blue house beside Mrs. Teasedale?" Alissa asked.

"Yes." Brad couldn't miss the faint glimmer of disapproval that flitted across Claire's face like a fading yet turbulent shadow.

"I'm Brad Ratner," he said. "And I belong to the smashed mailbox."

"You're the artist then?" Before Brad could nod, she continued. "I'm sorry. I sound like twenty questions. If you haven't already figured it out, I don't socialize much. I'm an overworked R.N." She tugged the collar of her nurse's uniform for emphasis. "Otherwise, I'd have introduced myself before now. Anyway, both Sarah Docker and Whit Jenkins told me when they sold their houses. The six of us whose yards meet in the back had all been neighbors for so long that, even though we didn't see a lot of each other, we made an effort to keep each other informed." Claire pushed her auburn curls from her forehead.

"I guess I've met everyone now except the man who lives on the other side of my house," Brad said, his mind skipping from Alissa's accident to what had occupied it since that morning: Who placed the bodies in his backyard?

"That's Richard Calbert. He . . . um . . . he's a little different," Claire said cautiously. "Different, but very nice."

"Oh," Brad said, not understanding what "different" meant to Claire Allen but at the same time not wishing to sound nosy.

"What do you mean by different?" Alissa

asked, apparently not caring who thought she was nosy. Brad covered an indulgent smile with his hand. He liked that in a woman. Curiosity. And plenty of it. With Alissa's inquisitive mind, he guessed her life would never be dull. She'd probably continuously ask questions that no one else had the guts to verbalize. Maybe his initial appreciation of her physical attractiveness had been brought about by this facet of her personality. Only a go-getter would spy over a backyard fence off and on all morning. Brad had seen her from the start. And what had begun in him as annoyance had turned into humor when he'd seen her obvious chagrin over her friend's blatant friendliness. Yes, Alissa was more curious than the average person but, surprisingly, she also was a bit shy. Just the right combination.

Dana had all the right combinations, too, an accusing voice whispered. Brad, his chest tightening, tried to ignore the taunting but knew deep within that the effort was hopeless.

"Well," Claire Allen continued in a lowered voice, "Richard's really not as strange as his — as he seems at first. He says he enjoys his job. Anyway, he makes decent money at it, they say. That's because he's so good at what he does. Maybe that's the strange part. That and the fact that it's odd for a middle-aged man. Most people in that profession are younger. But you'll know when you meet him, I guess, if you catch him on his way to work."

"Oh," Alissa said, sounding totally confused and in need of more information. Then she tensed and checked her watch. "For Pete's sake! I forgot my grandmother! It's six thirty now; I should have already been there!"

"I'll take you," Brad offered. "You can call your mechanic on your cell while I get my keys. Is there a chance he would tow it tonight and take a look at the brakes to see what happened?"

"Maybe. If he's not backed up with extra work. We're longtime friends — went to high school together. He usually makes room for me. I'm notorious for waiting till the last minute to have my car serviced, so his squeezing me in won't be the first time."

"Well, let me know if I can help," Claire said with a casual wave, and she walked back up the street.

Brad, waving to Claire, didn't voice his thoughts about Alissa's failed brakes. He did know enough about cars to understand that the brakes shouldn't have gone out if the maintenance check was done properly.

Perhaps finding those bones had made him overly suspicious, but something about her brakes failing bothered him. Just an unexplained shadow of uncertainty nibbling at the back of his mind. Uncertainty, which he hoped, was unfounded.

CHAPTER 6

"You're late!" Alissa's grandmother accused as she opened the front door of her petite brick home.

"I'm sorry. I was delayed." Licking her lips, Alissa hoped her grandmother wouldn't sense she was hiding something. Alissa's brakes "betraying" her would weigh so heavily on Emily Carrington's mind that she'd worry about it happening again. So Alissa had chosen to keep the wreck a secret, and instructed Brad to do likewise.

"I'm with a friend. I hope you don't mind," Alissa said, diverting her grandmother's attention to the white Lexus sitting in the driveway.

Just as Alissa had anticipated, the diversion worked. "Is it a man?" Emily hissed, peering from the doorway through her fashionable wire-rimmed glasses.

"Yes. Brad Ratner's his name. You saw him on television."

"Oh! The cute one!" Emily giggled. "Can't wait to meet him."

Even though Alissa had little choice in the turn of events, she wasn't so sure her grandmother meeting Brad was the best idea. Emily Carrington usually exposed Alissa's men friends to a barrage of personal questions.

Despite the questions, though, Alissa was thankful that her grandmother's mind was still as sharp as that of a woman half her age. Not only her mind, but her appearance, too. She insisted on up-to-date fashion, including a bobbed hairstyle, tasteful makeup, and Chanel designer suits. With her discreetly tinted brunette hair, sparkling blue eyes, and soft complexion, she would pass for sixty-five by anybody's standards. And as Alissa's grandmother handed her the infamous sweet potato casserole, Alissa had to admit her pride in being Emily Carrington's granddaughter. Even if she couldn't have the mother she longed for, at least she did have Grandma.

"I'll put this in the car while you lock up," Alissa said, holding up the casserole.

"Okay."

"Don't be surprised by what she asks you, Brad," Alissa mumbled as she placed the brown glass casserole dish on the floorboard behind his seat.

"Believe me, I won't." An impish smile lighted Brad's smoky eyes.

Alissa, returning the smile, left the back door open for her grandmother and took the front passenger seat.

Seconds later, Emily plopped into her place and lost no time waiting for introductions. "Hi. I'm Emily Carrington." She extended her hand between the bucket seats.

Brad shook the offered hand. "Nice to meet you, Mrs. Car—"

"None of that Mrs. Stuff, now. I'm Emily."

"Nice to meet you, Emily. I'm Brad Ratner."

"I know. I saw you on television. And you're a lot better lookin' than Alissa's last man friend."

"Grandma!" This was going to be even worse than Alissa had expected, bad enough to scald her cheeks.

"Well, it's the truth," Emily slammed the car door for emphasis.

Alissa didn't even bother to look at Brad. She didn't need to. His muffled snickers told her plainly that he was probably dying of hilarity.

"The church isn't far from here, Brad," Alissa said, willing her voice to be calm even though her heart was pounding in something akin to panic. "Down this street. Now take a right. It's about five miles ahead on the left." She gripped the edge of the tan leather car seat as if it were a cliff over which her grandmother was about to push her. "And you have my permission to break the speed limit," she whispered from the corner of her mouth.

"What do you do for a living?" Emily continued as if Alissa weren't present.

"I'm an artist."

"Oh," she said in disappointment. "I thought maybe you were a doctor or something. Alissa's last man friend was. Made good money, too. But he just wasn't the right one for her. I told her that from the start. He wasn't a churchgoing man. Are you?"

"What?" Brad asked.

"A churchgoing man."

"Well, um, I . . . yes, I have been."

Alissa suppressed the urge to clamp her hand over her grandmother's mouth. The subject of church was obviously an awkward one for Brad, and Alissa immediately thought of the dusty Bible in his living room. A Bible that spoke of a devout past. What had altered his devotion?

"Good, because Alissa's a fine Christian

girl. Do you know she even went to Africa last fall on a missions trip? Closed her clinic and everything, just to help those poor people over there with their teeth."

"Really?" Brad sounded genuinely impressed, and his warm glance looked it.

Alissa, on the other hand, was genuinely embarrassed. Once her grandmother started bragging, she might not stop.

"Yes, and she's planning on going back next summer," Emily continued.

"I'm sure Brad doesn't want to be bored with the details of my extracurricular activities," Alissa said, hoping to change the subject. Conversations in which she was the target of compliments always befuddled Alissa.

"On the contrary, I'm very interested," Brad said as he nearly leveled Alissa with his incredible smile.

She gripped the door's armrest and turned to gaze out the window at the city landscape mingled with majestic pines. Where would this acquaintance lead? Alissa had the expectant feeling of Christmas morning every time she looked at Brad, a feeling which had escalated into longing when he'd briefly embraced her after her accident.

"Do you make money with your artwork, Brad?" Emily asked.

"Yes." Brad's answer was laced with a chuckle.

"How much?"

"Grandma! You don't ask people questions like —"

"I do. Somebody's gotta look for you a good husband. Because let's face it, honey, you aren't doing too hot on your own."

Dismissing, or perhaps postponing, the money question, Emily clipped out her next query. "Have you ever been married?"

Alissa nearly choked. Emily hadn't asked Sherman that question until Alissa had been dating him a month. And she wasn't even dating Brad!

This time, though, Brad produced no mirthful snickers. His hands tightened on the steering wheel until his knuckles grew white. And silence enfolded them like the confining choke of death itself; the kind of icy, heavy silence that nobody, not even Emily Carrington, would dare break.

As the seconds ticked by and the car sped down the busy city street, Alissa waited breathlessly for his answer. She couldn't deny her own curiosity. She already knew he was hiding something painful from his past. Could it somehow involve marriage? And could this be the reason for his neglected Bible?

"Yes . . . once," he finally rasped. "She and my little girl . . . passed away two years ago."

"Oh, I see. I'm sorry, young man," Emily said discreetly, then changed the subject. "Have you checked on your clinic since you left Friday, Alissa?"

"No. I thought I might do that tomorrow. I need to check the voice mail anyway," Alissa said, wanting to applaud her grandmother. She had to give the woman credit for at least knowing when to end her prying questions.

"Don't you two worry about coming back to pick me up, now. I'll get that Reynolds man to take me home. He's been trying to get me to go for a ride in his new Corvette for weeks and weeks." She sighed. "Maybe if I go, he'll leave me alone."

"Mr. Reynolds is eighty," Alissa said as Brad pulled into the churchyard. "But he thinks he's forty."

"Forty!" Emily snorted. "More like sixteen! Do you know he actually thinks I'm going to date him?"

"Maybe you ought to think about it," Brad teased, his earlier tension vanishing. "It's a shame for an attractive woman like you not to have a boyfriend."

Alissa glanced toward her grandmother.

Emily's face remained impassive. "You know something? I like you," she said then opened the door to get out.

Minutes later, after Alissa helped Emily enter the church kitchen, she sat in the car, rolled her eyes, and shut the door. "I'm really sorry about her. I'm afraid she's a bit on the pushy side."

Brad's smile proved that Emily's questions hadn't caused him any real damage. "I didn't expect anything less," he teased. "After all, you're rather . . . inquisitive yourself. I figured you had to get it from somebody."

"Please tell me I'm not as bad as she is."

"I don't know . . ." Brad put the car in reverse and eased out into the road. "Spying on someone across a privacy fence is pretty . . . um . . ." He mockingly glanced up as if he were searching for the right word.

"Nosy, I believe is the term."

"Yes. As a matter a fact, you're right." Then, with a lopsided grin, Brad patted her shoulder and left his hand there several unnecessary seconds. Just long enough for Alissa to enjoy the effect. "But don't take it too hard. After all, something good came out of it. Without your nosiness we'd probably still be strangers."

"Oh, I doubt it," Alissa said. "You'd

undoubtedly have introduced yourself when I demolished your mailbox." But would it have been so bad for them to remain strangers?

She could get accustomed — really accustomed — to having Brad Ratner in her life. And Alissa didn't think that would be wise. He obviously still had strong feelings for his deceased wife. What warm-blooded human being wouldn't after only two years? Especially with his little girl dying, too. What a tragedy! Alissa couldn't stop herself from wondering how they died. A car wreck perhaps?

He'd made it very clear, however, that his past was none of her concern. Deciding the smart thing was to avoid him from now on, Alissa inhaled the smell of leather seats and watched the neighborhoods, grocery stores, and mall pass by. Avoiding him might be harder than she'd like to admit, though, especially since she didn't *want* to avoid him.

"Now I guess it's my turn to be nosy," he said. "Did you think that Mrs. Horton — what was her first name?"

"Sadie."

"Yeah. Did you think she was a little . . ."

"On the weird side?"

"Yeah."

"I thought she was a lot on the weird side. And I don't think Mrs. Teasedale is far behind her."

"You don't think . . . nah."

"What?" Alissa, eyes wide, looked at him, waiting for him to vocalize what she'd speculated all afternoon.

"Well, about those bones. Somebody had to put them in my backyard. And Mr. Jenkins swears it wasn't him."

"But do the police believe him?"

Brad shrugged. "At present, they seem to have no hard evidence against him."

Alissa toyed with the hem of her T-shirt. "Do you know if they've questioned Mrs. Docker yet?"

"No. I've never met her. What's she like?"

"The 'Granny Smith' type. Wouldn't hurt a fly. Or seemed like she wouldn't hurt a fly. I only met her in passing at the closing of my home purchase."

"But it's not flies we're talking about, is it?" Brad steered the Lexus into Alissa's circle driveway.

"You can say that again," she said. Opening the car door, she peered toward Brad's mailbox and was thankful to see her car had already been towed. As usual, Tom was at her beck and call. "I'll be interested in meeting Mr. Calbert. If he's as odd as Claire

Allen seems to think, he might be behind the bones. Did the police seem to have any leads on who could have been in your house?"

"No. But given my observations, they've narrowed it to probably being a female."

"Really? A woman?"

"Yes. Of average height and a slightly plump build. Either that or it was a man disguised as a woman."

"Or a thin woman who purposefully added some cushioning under her clothing." Alissa absently thought of Sadie Horton. Then she rolled her eyes. "Would you listen to me? A mere dentist, and I'm starting to sound like Alissa Carrington, private investigator."

"Yeah. And I'm no better. You just can't help but wonder, though." He took off his glasses and thoughtfully bit the earpiece.

"Well, maybe the police will find the murderer in a day or two, then close the investigation."

"For some reason, I don't think that's going to happen," he mumbled, as if his mind were no longer on the investigation.

His intense glance told Alissa exactly where his thoughts had traveled. It was the kind of mesmerizing, extended gaze that seemed to touch Alissa's very soul, incapacitating her. The effect verged on being hypnotic, almost as if she were falling into the smoky depths of his eyes. Then she was captive to a déjà vu feeling, as if their paths were destined to cross from the beginning of time.

But he only wanted friendship, and that was for the best. After all, Alissa wasn't sure she'd know true love if it bit her on the nose. She'd already devastated one man by mistaking human admiration for God-inspired love. She certainly didn't want to repeat that mistake, particularly not with a man as special as Brad Ratner. Alissa didn't think she could forgive herself for hurting Sherman, but she knew that she'd never forgive herself if she hurt Brad.

With a concentrated effort, she broke his disturbing gaze and turned to leave the car. "Well, um, thanks for the lift."

CHAPTER 7

"That's right," Tom said after Alissa returned his call. "The brake fluid line was cut."

Her palms sweaty, Alissa sank to her poster bed and clutched her comforter. "Someone — someone wanted me to wreck my car?" she croaked as her gray mutt padded in to the bedroom to stare up at her in canine curiosity. Alissa had let him in upon arriving home, half for his comfort and half for hers. Still shaken from the wreck, she hadn't wanted to be alone.

"It sure looks that way. I think it might be a good idea for you to report this to the police. I'm not sure there's anything they can do. That is, unless you've seen anyone strange around your place today."

"No, I haven't." Alissa thought of the person who'd run from Brad's house that afternoon, then dismissed him or her. That person had been prowling around Brad's property, not hers. Her brake line could have been cut last night while she was sleeping. And she'd learned an important lesson; she'd make doubly sure from now on that she locked her car in the garage instead of leaving it in the driveway. Her father had often scolded her for forgetting to lock it at night. She realized now that she should have listened.

"Anyway," Tom continued, "at least the police will file a report. Then if it happens to someone else in your neighborhood, maybe a pattern will develop and they can find out who did it. Sometimes this kind of thing can be traced to a sick kid with a perverted sense of humor."

"Yeah. Okay," Alissa managed to squeak out.

"Are you all right?" Tom asked, concern filling his soft voice.

"Do you want me to call the police for you, or come over or something?"

"No. I'll be okay." She really wanted to say yes. But at the same time Alissa didn't want to give Tom any reason for false romantic hope. He was an extremely attractive Christian man who owned a chain of successful auto repair and body shops that stretched from Fort Worth to Austin. Yet there was simply no spark there for Alissa.

She made arrangements for Tom's local garage to repair her Mustang, and was pressured to agree when he insisted on taking her to get a rental car the next day. A call to the police station produced a very sympathetic officer who, after a few questions, said exactly what Tom had speculated he might: Other than file a report, there was really nothing they could do at present.

Alissa then hovered over the phone, debating whether or not to call Brad. He'd requested that she let him know about her brake line, but that could wait until tomorrow. Besides, after her grandmother's pushiness, Alissa didn't want to give Brad the wrong idea and make him think she was chasing him.

So, in her desire for some human company, she decided to call her father who lived near Dallas, where he owned a pharmacy. She wouldn't worry him with the news of her brake line. The incident was probably what Tom had said — an impersonal prank.

"I hear you had a lunch date today," her father said after their initial greeting.

"Grandma didn't waste any time telling you, did she?" Alissa asked, flopping back on the bed to stare at the olive green and orange floral wallpaper with disgust. She

74

simply couldn't put off wallpapering her bedroom much longer.

"No. And she filled me in about the bones next door, too. I was going to call you tonight, but haven't had the chance yet. What's going on?" he said, his kind, soothing voice immediately easing Alissa's nerves.

He was going to make a wonderful grandfather to Alissa's children. That is, if she ever had any children. An empty longing which she continually suppressed nearly refused suppression at that moment. The option of a husband and children didn't seem to be unfolding at present. *What about Brad?* a tiny voice asked, inviting Alissa to fantasize about the possibility. But there was no reason to daydream about the unattainable.

Taking a deep breath, Alissa related the day's events to her father. "And regardless of what Grandma tells you, Brad Ratner and I are just friends," she ended.

"Brad Ratner!" her father exclaimed, his voice rising half an octave. "Your new neighbor isn't *the artist* Brad Ratner, is he?"

"Yes, he's an artist. Why do I feel like you know something I don't?" Alissa asked, sitting up. Her father, although not talented artistically, had always pursued his esthetic tastes, surrounding Alissa with original sculptures and valuable paintings while she was growing up. She often sensed he was secretly disappointed that his daughter hadn't inherited her mother's artistic talent. Oh, she appreciated beauty in art. She simply didn't have the consuming love for it that her parents had shared. Alissa had always preferred creating beauty with her flowers rather than a brush. That was the reason she bought Mrs. Docker's big old house. It had an equally big old yard that she could landscape and relandscape to her heart's content.

"Alissa dear, Brad Ratner is one of this decade's leading American artists. As young as he is, he's virtually a child prodigy. His last painting sold for a quarter of a million in France. The man is not only filthy rich, but he's also an artistic genius."

"Oh, my word," Alissa groaned, recalling Brad's conversation with her grandmother. The she fell back onto her pillows and placed her left hand to her forehead. "Guess what Grandma asked him when we went to pick her up tonight?"

"There's no telling."

"She asked if he made any money with his paintings. Then when he said yes, she asked how much."

Don Carrington snorted. "Did he tell her?"

"No! I cut her off before she could push the issue."

"Well, maybe meeting her will shock him into picking up the brush again. Word has it he hasn't painted one stroke in two years."

"Really?" Alissa couldn't hide her curiosity.

"Yes. Do you remember hearing about that random mass shooting two years ago at a fast-food restaurant in New York?"

Alissa racked her memory for the story. "I must have missed that one."

"Well, some idiot went in at lunchtime and slaughtered fourteen customers because he was mad at the manager for firing him. Anyway, Brad and his wife and daughter were there — I think their names were Dana and Kara. Brad got away with only a bullet wound, while his wife and daughter were killed."

Suddenly, several things about Brad clicked into place, his slight East Coast dialect. His awkwardly telling her he'd been involved in an "accident" two years ago. His understated class — that elusive quality that suggested near royalty to her, even when he wore faded jeans. Then there was his tangible pain over something from his past.

Now Alissa knew what that "something" was. No wonder he only requested friendship. The poor man was still recovering from the trauma of seeing his family murdered.

Could this be the reason for the dust on his Bible? Alissa remembered with aching clarity her initial anger at God when her mother died. She hadn't attended church for six months. Perhaps Brad felt the same way.

With a hard swallow, she vowed to honor Brad's request for a platonic relationship. As she'd sensed earlier, the last thing she needed to do was hurt him. That ruled out any romantic involvement because Alissa couldn't trust herself when it came to love. But she did know how to be a best friend. And she did know about turning to God in her pain, rather than blaming Him for it.

After another fifteen minutes of conversation, Alissa hung up with a promise that she'd introduce her father to Brad. She also felt much more at ease over her brake line having been sliced. Perhaps, as Tom had said, the cut was an incident hatched in the mind of some sick kid, and not an attack on her personally. With bones being unearthed next door, though, Alissa still had to resist the urge of looking over her shoulder every other second.

■ ■ ■ ■

She couldn't believe the watch was gone. She held the black knit pants upside down and shook them furiously, hoping she'd overlooked the earth-encrusted timepiece, which she'd placed in her pocket yesterday. Nothing fell from the pants, however, but a few pieces of dried soil. And she'd already searched the house.

All the trouble she'd gone through yesterday to retrieve the watch — running through Brad's house in broad daylight, knocking Louanne down — and she'd somehow lost the very thing for which she'd gone to the graveside, the very thing which could incriminate her as the murderer.

You fool! Why didn't you check your pockets yesterday afternoon as soon as you got home?

It was her memory. Henry mentioned only last week that he was concerned about her, that her short-term memory didn't seem as sharp as it had been. She'd been so consumed with having seen Louanne and "fixing" her car that all thoughts of the golden watch that she'd compulsively buried near the bodies ten years earlier had vanished. And, after taking off the black pants, she hadn't checked her pockets.

A decade ago she'd been so careful to cover her tracks. Why had she given into that momentary, grief-stricken urge to rid herself of the watch? Luckily, the pool company's digging hadn't unearthed it. They'd come within inches. She grinned. Maybe this was one more example of fate smiling on her. No one had suspected her crime ten years before because of fate's willful cooperation.

The momentary smug smile turned into a rebellious scowl. Now the watch was gone. Fate must have turned against her. Furiously tugging the pants pockets wrong side out, she saw the hole for the first time. The hole was just big enough for the watch to have slipped and fallen to the ground. A frustrated shriek erupted from her soul, and she threw the pants across the bedroom to land on the row of crystal perfume bottles lining the mahogany dresser. Then, with an agile forward lunge, she violently raked the pants and perfume bottles onto the floor in a heap of shattering glass. Nothing was going right. First, Louanne didn't die as planned, now the watch.

Her momentary fury spent, she collapsed onto the queen-sized brass bed to stare at the ceiling. She must retrace her steps through the neighborhood. Maybe Richard Calbert would help her once more. After all, he'd assisted her when she buried the bodies.

CHAPTER 8

Trying to ignore the green wallpaper, Alissa slipped on her cotton garden gloves and left her bedroom. Yes, she was putting off the wallpapering project again. But today's weather was identical to yesterday's — not a cloud in sight. And the early morning coolness beckoned her to work outdoors. She planned to remove the boring monkey grass from the front flowerbed near her driveway and replace it with some pink geraniums. The weatherman had predicted rain for this afternoon. Maybe she'd start the wallpapering then.

Ten minutes later, her remodeling project forgotten, Alissa overturned shovel after shovel full of moist earth, then began removing the monkey grass from its flowerbed. For every clump she set aside, though, Frito created four or five clumps. He'd appointed himself her official "assistant gardener" when he was a puppy, and Alissa never denied him the joy of "helping" her.

"That mutt of yours is spoiled rotten" was one of her grandmother's favorite lines. It was the absolute, unadulterated truth, though. Alissa, tossing a new clump of monkey grass into the air, playfully tweaked the dog's ear before he ran around the yard in a frantic circle, the grass hanging from his teeth. He enjoyed the 6:30 a.m. coolness and the fragrant smell of dew-laden pines as much as she did.

As she shook the third large clump of grass free of soil, however, something other than dirt fell from the grass. Something heavy enough to make a metallic clink as it hit the flowerbed's brick border. Something, although caked in soil, resembled a very expensive, diamond-studded gold watch. Either that or it was a cheap fake a child had lost during play.

Picking up the watch, Alissa rubbed her gloved thumb over the face to dislodge some of the dirt. That revealed what she'd originally suspected. The watch was one of the most expensive brands available. Standing now, she wondered what she should do with it. Run a "lost and found" ad in the paper? Or maybe call Mrs. Docker? Perhaps the watch was hers.

"Good morning," a pleasant male voice

called from her driveway. Turning, Alissa encountered a tall, thin jogger, probably in his late forties, who was wearing black-and-white running gear and a welcoming smile. His tan spoke of many hours outdoors, as did his sandy, sun-streaked hair.

"Good morning," she called back as he jogged into her yard to stop a few feet away.

"I'm Richard Calbert. I live two houses down. I saw you out this morning and just thought I'd introduce myself," he said through puffs of air.

"Alissa Carrington," she said, starting to extend her hand, only to stop with a wry smile. "I guess we'd better not shake. That is, unless you want to get your hands dirty."

The corners of his hazel eyes crinkled as his grin increased, and he grabbed her gloved hand and shook it firmly. "A little dirt never hurt anyone."

"That's always been my motto," Alissa agreed, wondering what Claire Allen found so weird about this man. He looked and talked perfectly normal.

"I'm sorry I haven't gotten around to introducing myself sooner, but I've been busy with my business. It keeps me hoppin'."

"Oh?" Alissa said, inviting him to expound on exactly what business he was in. Claire

Allen had left no doubts it was something strange, at least in her eyes.

"Yes. I own a couple of flower and greetings shops. I have florists who do the arranging. I'm in charge of the greetings. Sometimes I'm a singing gorilla, sometimes Tarzan himself." He shrugged, his kind eyes twinkling with mirth. "It all depends on what the customers order."

"Oh yeah, I know you! I've seen your advertisements on television. You're dressed as a trapeze artist."

"That's me," he said. "One time . . ." His spontaneous laughter interrupted his words. "A couple of years back, someone had me dress as a ballerina for a gag. It was hilarious. Claire Allen saw me," he pointed toward Claire's house, "and I don't think she's gotten over it yet. She thought I was a tad bit on the strange side already, I guess. But that just pushed her opinion over the edge. Quite frankly" — he lowered his voice in mock seriousness — "I sometimes think she's a bit weird herself. Anyone who would raise goldfish so her cat can have fresh cuisine . . ." He rolled his eyes. "I've lived here fifteen years. They were all here when I moved in except for Mrs. Docker." He waved toward Sadie, Elizabeth, Claire, and Brad's houses. "Mrs. Docker bought your

85

house ten years ago. Anyway, I'd thought for a long time that my only normal neighbors were Sarah Docker and Whit Jenkins."

Alissa giggled, her heart warming to this cheerful man. She could clearly understand how someone as serious-looking as Claire would think someone as lighthearted and chatty as Richard could be a bit odd.

"And from what I understand from the neighborhood gossip, you're a dentist, right?" he continued.

"Yes. It doesn't take long to travel, does it?"

"Not in this neighborhood. Sometimes I think Mrs. Teasedale and Mrs. Horton know my business before I do. For instance, yesterday evening when I got home, I had a message on my machine from Mrs. Teasedale about the bones in Brad Ratner's backyard. They've been highly interested because of Brad's fame as a painter."

"Oh?" Alissa began to wonder if everyone but her had prior knowledge of Brad's career.

"Yeah. Anyway, I think this bones business is kind of chilling, don't you?"

"That's an understatement. It's amazing to me that something like human bones could be unearthed in such a quiet neighborhood."

Alissa absently glanced at the earth-encrusted watch and rubbed the face with her thumb. "You wouldn't happen to know who this belongs to, would you? I just found it in my flowerbed. Did Mrs. Docker own a watch like this?" She extended it forward.

Richard, whistling softly, took it from her. "This cost a hunk of money. I don't think Mrs. Docker would have splurged on something like this. She's a widow on a fixed income, and besides that, she's eternally thrifty."

"I was thinking about putting an ad in the paper. I'm sure the owner would be glad to have the watch returned."

"Good idea. Incidentally, my brother's a jeweler, owns Calbert Jewelry downtown." Alissa nodded, recognizing the reputable name. "Why don't you take it by his place and have him dissect it and clean it up? He'll even appraise it for you. Then you'll better know what you're dealing with. You don't want to have the ad answered by some swindler who can take advantage of you because you don't have all the facts. I'll tell you what," he said, never taking a breath. "I'll take it to him, if you'll let me. That way, he won't charge you. He owes me anyway. I dressed up like a giant rooster for him last week. He'd wanted me to catch his salesclerk off guard and give her a big birthday kiss. I wound up chasing the poor woman down the street. Scared her to death at first, I think. Anyway, by the time I caught her, both of us, and a whole city block of onlookers were doubled up with laughter. So, like I said, he owes me."

"Okay," Alissa said with a chuckle, then immediately questioned her hasty decision. She'd only just met Richard Calbert. What if he were a swindler? She might never see the valuable watch again. Another glance into his hazel eyes swept away all doubts. If Richard Calbert were dishonest, then so was apple pie and motherhood.

With a satisfied smile, she walked away from the large oak she'd been hiding behind in order to eavesdrop on Richard and Louanne's conversation. Louanne had never seen her watching from the yard's outer boundary, never known that Richard Calbert was once again assisting the person who'd murdered her. The person who'd murder her again, very, very soon.

From his kitchen window, Brad watched as Alissa bade good-bye to Richard Calbert. He'd met the Calbert man yesterday after taking Alissa home. They'd pulled into their

driveways simultaneously and had introduced themselves. Richard seemed nice
enough — not quite as weird as Claire Allen
had depicted him, not quite as nosy as Sadie
Horton, Elizabeth Teasedale, or even Claire
herself. He'd been only slightly curious
about Alissa's accident as Brad briefly told
him the details.

At the moment, though, Brad dismissed
the thoughts of Mr. Calbert and concentrated on Alissa. He'd left the message on
her machine yesterday evening because he'd
wanted to ask her opinion about a painting.
Later he decided that was foolish, perhaps a
mere ploy for her attention. But he couldn't
deny that his interest in his work, once a
driving passion, seemed to be returning.

Something about Alissa ignited a need in
his soul he'd considered completely dead.
Perhaps it was her high cheekbones, her full
lips, or her slightly square jawline, or maybe
the combination of all three. But whatever
the cause, the end result was the same. Brad
had the undeniable desire to sketch her
profile.

"Forget her profile," he mumbled, Brad
really wanted to create a full-blown portrait
of the woman enjoying her favorite pastime,
her flowers. Giving into the compulsion, he
raced to his bedroom closet, flung it open,

and reached to the back of the highest shelf, where he'd stashed his sketch pad. Only yesterday he had wondered if he'd ever feel the creative urge again. Now he knew.

With a fervor he hadn't felt in two years, he flipped open the pad, grabbed one of his sketching pencils, and rushed back to the kitchen window.

In Brad's exultation, the pencil began moving over the paper as if of its own accord. This feeling, this experience, was exactly the same as it had always been. The heat of the moment; the intense force that refused denial; the churning within that sought release, a release only achieved with the finished work of art. Genius, some called it, but Brad called it creation.

Then, as Alissa's shoulder-length hair, captivating almond-shaped eyes, and cute pug nose flowed from pencil to paper, guilt flowed through his being. What was he doing? Had he lost his mind? What about Dana?

Every morning since her death, he'd awakened with her in his heart, in his mind. Blinking, he stared at the porcelain sink as a sickening realization seared through him; he hadn't even thought of her this morning. This morning, he'd awakened wondering what plans Alissa had for the day, hoping their paths would cross, planning an "accidental" encounter.

He tried to revive Dana's smiling face in his mind, tried to obliterate Alissa's. But he couldn't. He couldn't even remember what Dana looked like. The counselor had suggested he move to another city, start a new life for himself; had said a move might be the key to his recovery from that . . . that holocaust he'd witnessed. Could he, after two years, finally be recovering?

His upper lip broke out in clammy beads of perspiration, the sweat quickly moved to his forehead and trailed down his spine. But where did that leave Dana? And little Kara?

"No-o-o!" he screamed. Turning, he hurled the sketch pad toward the oak breakfast bar. Samantha, who'd been contentedly sleeping on one of the bar chairs, jumped and scampered into the living room, her tail straightened.

Brad wanted to run just as Samantha had, wanted to flee from the emotions which were tying his very soul into a knotted mass of confusion. He marched to the bar, retrieved the rejected sketchpad, and with new determination, ripped the offending drawing into four pieces. God might have turned His back on Dana and Kara in His "wis-

91

dom," failing to protect them, but Brad would never turn his back on them.

He'd decided yesterday that he must remain faithful to Dana. That decision stayed firm. Regardless of his emotions, regardless of Alissa's magnetic femininity, her mass of honey-colored hair, or her fabulous figure, he and Alissa Carrington would never be anything more than friends. Period! He dropped the torn sketch into the nearby trash basket.

The front doorbell's ringing seemed to finalize his decision. When he opened the door, however, he momentarily wondered if his betraying heart had conjured up its desire despite his head's persistent wish.

"I'm terribly sorry to bother you, Brad," Alissa said, her brown eyes pleading for understanding. "And I know it's early, but could you give me a lift? I had a call from a patient just now — infected wisdom teeth. If he weren't in excruciating pain, I'd wait on a taxi. Anyway, I could use a ride to the clinic as soon as possible. Would you mind?"

"I'd be glad to give you a lift," he heard himself say despite the guilt, the warning bells penetrating his mind. And once again, regardless of his fighting to keep it alive, Dana's memory faded from his thoughts.

CHAPTER 9

"I hate to tell you this, Barry," Alissa said to the twenty-year-old Oriental college student after examining his teeth, "but it looks like your wisdom teeth are going to have to come out. Your gums are infected right now, though. That's the reason you're having the pain. I'm surprised you could even swallow. The swelling has even gone down into your throat."

"It wasn't really bad until yesterday. Then this morning, when I woke up . . ." He rolled his eyes to punctuate the pain.

Removing the blue examination mask, Alissa held up the X-rays for him to see. "These are really impacted. I could extract them, but you'll have less pain if you go to an oral surgeon and let him put you under anesthesia. While you're having the bottom ones out, I'd go ahead and have the surgeon take the top ones out, too." She pointed to the white teeth visible above his dark gum line as the antiseptic smell of her examination room seemed to support her diagnosis. "You don't have enough jaw space for them to drop properly. And you're just putting off the inevitable if you don't go ahead and have them taken care of. I'm going to write you a prescription for an antibiotic to get rid of the infection. Then I'll make you an appointment with Dr. Gardner for next week. In my opinion, he's the best oral surgeon in the area."

"Okay, thanks, Dr. Carrington. Oh, and thanks for coming in during your vacation. I'm sorry to have bothered you at home," Barry said, looking at her gratefully. "I — I hope I didn't interrupt anything, um . . . important." He glanced at the doorway meaningfully.

Following his gaze, Alissa reached for her prescription pad and saw Brad, arms crossed, watching from the room's doorway. His serious smoky eyes reflected something akin to admiration. Then, he looked down.

Barry must have noticed Brad's expression and assumed . . . only he knew what!

"Oh no, Barry, you didn't interrupt anything," she rushed, her betraying cheeks growing decisively warmer. "He's just, we're — we're just — this is my neighbor, Brad Ratner. He gave me a lift because my car's

94

in the shop." If she sounded half as flustered and guilty to Barry as she did to herself, she'd probably done nothing but reinforce his assumptions. Brad's quick silent retreat didn't do much to lessen the impression, either.

Alissa, concentrating on writing the prescription, tried to pretend the situation didn't exist. And, with a hard swallow against the sudden lump in her throat, she attempted to regain her professional composure.

Why did Brad have to be so attractive? Even in his glasses, which he now wore, he looked like something out of a magazine. Well, maybe not quite that perfect. But close enough to make Alissa want to stand back and observe him in feminine admiration.

Apparently even Barry sensed the undercurrent of attraction Alissa felt for Brad. And if Barry could see it, what did Brad see? *Friends, friends, friends. We can only be friends,* she repeated to herself as she made the appointment for Barry's surgery, took the young man's payment, and bade him good-bye.

She and Brad had barely spoken on the way to the clinic. The atmosphere between them could only be described as strained, something Alissa didn't understand. Last night, she'd felt perfectly comfortable in his presence. Perhaps he wasn't a morning person, or didn't appreciate being disturbed so early. Or maybe, after being grilled by her grandmother, he'd decided he didn't even want her friendship anymore. But then there was that certain . . . light in his eyes when he looked at her, the same light that Barry must have noticed.

"I'm just going to check my voice mail and make sure everything's okay in the other examination rooms before leaving, Brad," she called into the waiting room.

"Okay. No rush," he called back.

There were nothing but routine messages in her voice mail. And as Alissa rounded the corner to enter the back examination room, what she saw hanging outside the window completely obliterated those messages from her mind.

"Brad!" she croaked, rushing into the waiting room. "Someone — someone — there's something in here . . ."

"What is it? Are you all right?" His eyes wide, he jumped to his feet and rushed to Alissa's side.

Alissa instinctively covered her eyes, trying to wipe the image from her mind, but it was no use. "Just — just go look," she breathed and pointed down the hall. "Last door — on the left."

Brad rushed to the back room with Alissa following at a more cautious pace.

"This is sick," he said seconds later as he stared at the window.

"I know. It looks almost exactly like Frito, doesn't it?" Alissa's lips quivered as she peered at the life-sized stuffed dog that hung by its neck from a white cord just outside the window. "At first, I thought it — it was him."

After the initial shock, the stuffed animal hadn't been what turned Alissa's stomach, though. The message taped to the window was what had sent her running in fear. A simple piece of notebook paper, that's all. But the words "You're next. Don't think you'll survive again!" meticulously cut and pasted from newsprint, had made her nauseous, made her nauseous still.

And the worst part of all, a snapshot of Alissa's car smashed against Brad's mailbox hung just beneath the words.

"Last — last night my mechanic said — said the brake line was cut," Alissa stammered in a quivering voice. "He seemed to think — think it was an impersonal prank by some kid. But —"

"There's nothing impersonal about this," Brad stated. "We need to call the police."

"But I want to go back home and check on Frito. What if they try to kill him while I'm gone?"

"Look," Brad said, turning to grab her shoulders in an intense grip. "As much as I love animals, Frito is only a dog. You, on the other hand, are a human being. You need to call the police now. This world has its share of sickos — people who kill innocent women and children without so much as a blink." His gray eyes deepened to black pools of despair as his fingers' tightening grip bit into her shoulders. "And I won't simply stand by while someone kills you. Do you understand?" he almost shouted.

Alissa stood speechless, as his gaze seemed to paralyze her.

Then, his fingers relaxing, some of the intensity faded from his eyes. "I'm overreacting, aren't I?"

Alissa nodded, understanding full well why he was overreacting. If, like her father said, Brad had witnessed his wife and daughter's murder, she'd probably have reacted just as strongly if she were Brad.

"You're right, though. I'll call the police. And when they leave, we'll go check on Frito."

"I'm sorry," he said, touching her cheek

98

with the back of his index finger. "It's just that —"

"I understand," she whispered, slowly reaching up to cover his hand with hers. This time, however, Alissa felt no chills, no tingles from their close contact. Instead, she experienced a "coming home" feeling, a feeling which said her hand belonged, had always belonged, in Brad's. *Oh, dear God, is he the one?*

As the moment stretched, Brad's gaze traveled from her eyes to her lips, to linger there with naked longing glimmering like the faint flame of a newly lighted candle.

Then the tingles came, sweeping from Alissa's abdomen up her chest and on to her lips. Tingles. Or the conquering tide of desire long held at bay.

Then, a denying wind snuffed the flame from Brad's eyes; it was replaced by the determined set of his lips and a measured, backward step. "Go call the police," he said and abruptly turned away. "I'm going to check on the window from the outside."

"You can think of no one who could possibly have a vendetta against you, Dr. Carrington?" the African-American police officer asked some thirty minutes later. "An ex-patient, perhaps?"

"No, no one," Alissa said, watching through the window as the policewoman liberally applied black powder on the glass pane. She'd taken several snapshots, then removed the stuffed animal and message. Now she was checking for prints.

"Well, unless Lieutenant Peterson finds any prints, there's really not much we can do. And it's not like it is on TV. Most of the time we don't find any prints."

"Yeah. That's about what I figured," Alissa said dully.

"I'm sorry," he replied. "But . . ." With a helpless shrug he stared at the report he'd been filling out. "You just need to be careful. Do you have someplace you could go to stay awhile?"

"Why?" Alissa shrugged and tugged on the hem of her oversized pink cotton shirt. "If this person is really intent on harming me, which, judging by the seriousness of yesterday's crime, I assume he is" — she gave way to an undeniable shudder — "then won't he resume his campaign when I come back? I can't hide the rest of my life. I've got a practice to run, for starters." She waved her arm toward the front office.

"I know it's difficult, but . . ." he trailed off, obviously accepting defeat when he saw it.

Alissa suppressed the tears of frustration stinging her eyes and stared out the window at the policewoman still dusting for prints. Brad, standing behind the policewoman, peered over her shoulder, his face full of unasked questions. He had barely glanced at Alissa since the breathless moment when he'd almost kissed her. Alissa hadn't looked at him much either. She knew in her head that their relationship shouldn't develop beyond friendship. Her heart, however, was another story. Her heart had wanted nothing more than to feel his lips on hers.

CHAPTER 10

Alissa didn't say a word on the short drive home. She couldn't. Her mind was focused on what she'd find when she opened her backyard gate. Frito hanging by his neck? He'd wanted to stay in the house when she left for the clinic, but she had forced him outside. Had she forced him into the jaws of death?

Seeming to sense her despair, Brad remained respectfully quiet. "Would you like me to go inside with you?" he asked as he slowly turned into her circular driveway.

Nodding approval, Alissa glanced at him in appreciation. "Would you mind?"

Brad's answer never came. Instead, he slammed on his brakes. "Do you know that car?" he shouted, pointing toward the red Mercedes sitting in the drive.

Because the vast array of trees and shrubbery partially blocked her view of the driveway, Alissa hadn't noticed the car until now. Her heart skipped in reaction to Brad's reaction. Then she relaxed. "Yes. It's Tom McDaniel. My mechanic. He promised to arrange for a rental car for me last night when he gave me the report on my car. I guess that's what he's here for."

Brad's tense expression vanished. "Sorry. I'm a little jumpy," he said as Tom unfolded his tall, thin frame from the Mercedes. "Did he tell you last night that your brake line had been cut?" He drove the remaining few feet of driveway, then smoothly stopped the automobile and turned off the purring engine.

"Yes."

"Why didn't you call and let me know?"

"Well . . ." Alissa didn't know exactly what to say. She hadn't called because, at that moment, she hadn't wanted to appear pushy. Hadn't wanted him to think she, like her grandmother, saw him as nothing more than matrimony material.

Tom, however, saved her from a reply when he gallantly opened Alissa's door. "I just drove up," he said, his ginger-colored eyes alight with a welcoming smile. "Perfect timing, huh?"

"Yeah. Thanks for coming," she said, tensely grabbing her purse and stepping from the car. "If you'll wait just a minute,

103

I'll be ready to go. But first, I've — I've got to check something." Frito. Was her best buddy still alive?

Frito himself answered that question, though, when he raced from Brad's front yard with Samantha close on his heels. Alissa sank against the car, her eyes watering with relief.

Brad, now at her side, placed his hand on her shoulder. "Looks like you didn't have anything to worry about," he soothed.

"Thank God." She dropped to her knees and whistled. "Frito! Come here, boy!" Alissa winced against the impact of concrete on her sore knees. Even the Band-Aids didn't cushion the blow enough to ease the pain.

"What's going on?" Tom asked.

"I received a nasty threat at the clinic," Alissa said, hating the words even as she said them. "Someone hung a stuffed dog that looked like Frito outside the exam room and left a message that said I would be next." Her deep breath shook despite her wish to control it. "Anyway, I was worried about what I'd find when I got home."

Frito, noticing Alissa for the first time, lowered his tail and ears. He completely ignored Samantha, who playfully attacked his right hind leg, and made a mad dash for the backyard.

Alissa forced a chuckle, and also forced her voice to a cheerful calm as she stood. "He knows he's not supposed to be out of the backyard. He keeps digging holes under the fence. I had to discipline him last week for it. He's going to get himself run over."

"Alissa." Tom, ignoring her attempt at cheerfulness, placed a protective arm around her shoulders. "Why don't you stay with Mother for a few weeks? She'd love to have you, and the Florida coastline would probably do you good."

Brad's quick, perceptive glance took in first Alissa then Tom, and she felt the need to explain that Tom's affection was not reciprocated. But why did she owe Brad an explanation? She'd only just met the man, for Pete's sake.

"Thanks for the offer, Tom, but I can't run. Let me make sure everything's okay inside; then we'll go for the rental car," Alissa blurted out, wanting to change the subject. Tom's constant offer of assistance was painfully apparent. She'd thought when it started six months ago that her continued refusals would politely hint at her lack of interest. His tall, trim frame, boy-next-door auburn hair, easy smile, and financial security would probably be many a woman's dream come true. But not Alissa's.

"Oh. I decided to let you use my car," Tom said. "I've got the Volkswagen I can beat around in until I finish with your Mustang. The Mercedes is new and I'd rather you be in something I know is safe than take a chance on a rental car."

"But —"

"No buts." Tom extended the car's two keys to her.

"As far as that goes," Brad said evenly, his eyes a mask of something unreadable, something that may have bordered on a challenge, "Alissa always has a ride with me. She could even borrow my car, if she likes."

Tom looked Brad square in the eyes, a look much like a bull that's been defied by an equal match. "I don't believe we've been introduced," he said and extended his hand. "I'm Tom McDaniel, a longtime friend of Alissa's. And you're . . . ?" The greeting, although "proper" in form, sounded more like a territorial claiming of property.

"Brad Ratner." A tight smile. "Alissa's new neighbor and friend. I live right there." He pointed to his sprawling house. "So like I said, it will be no trouble for me to play chauffeur for a few days."

Alissa felt like a heifer being auctioned off to the highest bidder, a feeling she didn't appreciate. "Thanks, but no thanks to both of you," she said. "I'd rather have my own rental car. The last thing I need right now is to worry about getting a scratch on a Mercedes or whether or not my . . . chauffeur is home."

The muffled ringing of Tom's cell phone stopped him from protesting Alissa's decision. "Okay," he said, turning to the car. "But I still say you should leave town for a while."

"He might be right," Brad said, scowling at Tom as he answered the phone in the car. "Do you have a relative somewhere you could stay with?"

Exhaling, Alissa glanced at him, noting the glint of concern in his eyes, a concern also evident in his voice. "That sounds good, but what happens when I come back home?" she asked. "It would probably just start up again. And if this person is really after me, then how do I know he won't follow me out of town?"

"You don't, I guess," he said with resignation. "But I just don't want to stand by and watch —"

"That was the body shop here in town," Tom said, walking toward them. "I've got an irate customer who refuses to deal with the manager. So I've got to go." He looked at Alissa, his eyes beseechingly kind. "Are you sure you won't take the Mercedes? I really wouldn't mind."

"No," Alissa said in her most decisive yet most considerate voice. "A rental car will be fine."

"Okay. Well, I'll take care of this customer then be back to drive you to get a car."

"I'll take her," Brad offered quickly. "I'm not busy at the moment anyway."

"It must be nice," Tom muttered, his voice cloaked with the resentment of a possessive seventeen-year-old. "Don't you have to work for a living?"

Brad's jaws clenched, and Alissa placed her hand on Tom's arm. Tact wasn't one of Tom's better qualities, especially not when he was annoyed, and Brad obviously did annoy him. Alissa suspected, however, that the feeling was mutual.

"I'm sorry you can't stay, Tom," she said pointedly. "But I know how demanding your job is."

"Yeah . . . right," he muttered, his stony gaze softening as it turned from Brad to Alissa. "I'll call you later." And with that, he slid into his car, cranked the diesel engine, and drove away.

"How long did you say you've known him?" Brad asked.

"Since high school."

"Why do you put up with him?"

"He's usually not like this. He's really a fine Christian man."

"Well, he's the kind of guy that gets on my nerves."

Barely able to hide her smile, Alissa said, "I think he feels the same about you . . . um, would you mind going inside with me? I just want to make sure everything's okay before we go," she added, discreetly trying to change the subject. Part of her was elated that Tom seemed to evoke a certain jealousy in Brad. The other part, however, wanted to skirt the issue. Jealousy usually came equipped with romantic motivation, something Alissa wasn't sure of in her or Brad.

"I'm going to have a banana on the way. Want one, Brad?" Alissa asked ten minutes later after she and Brad had glanced through the house, and, much to her relief found everything exactly as she'd left it. She'd also locked Frito snugly into the glassed-in sunroom leading onto her patio. No sense in taking any chances with his life. Alissa plucked a banana for herself from the ripening bunch on top of the refrigerator.

"No, thanks," Brad said. "I never have cared for bananas. Besides, I'm still full from breakfast."

"As far as I'm concerned, anyone who doesn't like bananas must be a space alien," she teased, not mentioning that the piece of fruit was her breakfast.

"I'm not so sure you're not the space alien," he parried. "I didn't know dentists stopped their vacation to see patients. That was really admirable of you."

"Oh," she said, trying to formulate a practical reason for so readily allowing a patient to interrupt her free time. "Well, his family's been my and Trena's patients since we opened the clinic five years ago. So I figured I owe it to him. Trena would have done the same thing if she'd been here, I'm sure. Besides, it didn't take that long."

"Regardless, it was still thoughtful."

Alissa, never knowing how to react to compliments, studied the banana and searched for something to say. "Thanks," she finally squeaked out. She really hadn't given the emergency dental exam any thought and was at a loss to think someone considered it generous.

"Uh . . . Alissa . . ." Brad paused awkwardly and rubbed the nape of his neck where his straight hair touched his white cotton shirt's collar.

Her finger suddenly itched to touch his

hair, to feel its softness against her fingers. Instead, she concentrated on nonchalantly peeling her banana and nibbling the sweet fruit. After today, she vowed to herself, she would stay away from the man because her mind defied taming when he was near.

"I wanted to ask you something," he continued. "Earlier, when we were at the clinic and I got carried away, you said you understood why I'd reacted like I did. And I felt that you did understand much more than I've told you. You know about Dana and Kara, don't you?"

She swallowed the bit of banana in a nervous gulp. "Yes." A dry cough. "Um . . . my father, he . . . um, he's a big fan of yours. A real art connoisseur. Anyway, when I was on the phone with him last night, he told me about — about the shooting." With this explanation, she felt just as nosy and prying as Mrs. Teasedale.

"Did he tell you I haven't painted in two years, then?"

"Um, yes," Alissa shamefully said to the drooping banana peel and then cautiously glanced at him.

One corner of his lips tilted in a smile — part force, part genuine. "Did he also know the reason that I moved to Tyler?"

"No, he, um . . . he didn't go into that."

"Well, I'll tell you, then. It was an attempt to start a new life for myself. You know, to stop living in the past and create a 'bright future.' " He waved his hand in sarcasm. "My sister owns a farm an hour from here. So I thought, why not?"

"Is it — do you think it's going to work?" Alissa had never felt so awkward, so stupid, in her whole life. What a dumb thing to ask a man who's seen his family murdered.

"Who knows?" he said, a bitter twist to his mouth.

"Um, Brad, I — I don't want to pry, but . . ." Alissa nervously licked her lips as she mentally prepared her next words, words that would answer a question and perhaps simultaneously give him hope. "Well, my mother died when I was fifteen, and I was furious with God for a long time after that." She shrugged uncertainly and hoped she wasn't prying. "I don't know if it will help you or not, but I finally realized that God was there to comfort me in my pain. All I had to do was turn to Him."

"God?" he exploded, his eyes churning gray clouds. "I'll tell you about God! I went to church my whole life, did my best to live a Christian life, then He repaid me by killing my family!"

"Oh no, Brad," Alissa whispered. "God

didn't kill them."

"He could have stopped it, and He didn't!" he yelled. "That's the same thing as killing them to me."

She stared at him in helpless silence, a silence that stretched between them like a great, gaping canyon. Yes, her words had answered the question his dust-covered Bible had raised. Unlike Sherman, Brad was a Christian, but he was struggling for his spiritual health.

With a sigh, Brad scrubbed his fingers through his hair as if he wanted to pull it out by the roots. "I'm — I'm sorry. I shouldn't have taken my frustration out on you. If it's any consolation, the last couple of days haven't given me as much time to think about the past. Between the bones in my backyard and all your upheaval . . ."

"I, uh, guess I have kept you quite busy, haven't I?"

"More than you know," he mumbled, his eyes growing very serious and then taking on that guarded wariness she'd seen at the clinic.

Alissa swallowed again as an undeniable attraction sprang between them. But Brad turned toward the living room. "I'm ready to go when you are," he said bluntly.

Frustration. Alissa had never felt it so

sharply, so poignantly, as her stomach twisted into a tight wad of tension. Brad seemed to be making a career of saying and doing heart-stopping things, then cutting the moment short.

She placed the unfinished banana on the kitchen counter, took a deep breath, and grabbed a bottled water from the fridge. Alissa needed a long, cool drink of water to calm her nerves, and then she'd go rent herself a car. After that, she'd avoid Brad as if he had the plague. Forget his friendship business. Alissa wasn't prepared for the emotional hurricane in which he seemed determined to keep her.

The doorbell's soft chime punctuated her decision. The visitors who greeted her, however, momentarily erased all thoughts of Brad's contradictory behavior and replaced them with thoughts of intrigue.

CHAPTER 11

"We just stopped by for a moment to welcome you to the neighborhood properly. We were afraid we didn't make the best impression yesterday and wanted to apologize." Mrs. Teasedale, again wearing her pink sponge rollers and bright orange lipstick, stepped into the foyer, with Mrs. Horton close behind. Both ladies stared curiously at Brad who stood beside one of the mauve, wing-backed chairs.

Alissa smiled in appreciation for the homemade bread Mrs. Horton soberly extended toward her. "Thank you. Would you like to sit down?"

"No, no, we can't," Sadie said, her rough voice much more congenial than it had been yesterday, her Lucille Ball red hair just as unkempt. "Henry's waiting in the car."

As she snapped the front door shut, Alissa sneaked a peek at the decade-old silver Cadillac purring in the driveway. The man behind the wheel was indistinguishable. Alissa was curious about the kind of person who'd marry someone like Sadie Horton, obviously not a man who pursued a woman of winning personality. Sadie, although attempting to act pleasant today, still appeared more brusque than neighborly.

"We heard about your accident yesterday," Sadie said. "How'd it happen?"

Mrs. Teasedale, apparently more inclined to display proper manners, elbowed Sadie in the ribs. "What she's tryin' to say, Dr. Carrington," she began in her heavy Texan dialect, "is that we wanted to thank you for coming to help when I fell off the ladder yesterday."

"How is your ankle, by the way?" Alissa asked.

"All better. The doctor said I just wrenched it, so it's only a tad bit sore." She flexed her ankle. "We came over, though, because we were terribly sorry to hear about your accident. We wanted to check in on you to make sure you weren't injured and wondered if there was anything we could do?" Although her words were right, her eyes depicted a lack of interest.

Elizabeth Teasedale seemed more concerned with examining the interior of Alissa's home than with offering assistance to an accident victim.

"Someone cut Alissa's brake line," Brad explained, walking up behind Alissa to take her right elbow.

"Really?" Sadie exclaimed sounding truly astonished. Or was that feigned astonishment? Something about that scrawny woman made Alissa's skin feel as if it were shriveling.

"That's terrible!" Mrs. Teasedale gasped, putting her fingertips to her mouth. Her nails were painted a bright orange and perfectly matched her lips. As with her condolences for the accident, her blue gaze wasn't on Alissa. Instead, she focused on Brad's hand as it gripped Alissa's elbow.

Alissa, trying to deny the tingles, purposefully pulled away from him. This was exactly the kind of contradictory behavior that was driving her crazy. One minute he almost ignored her, the next, he acted as if he had some claim on her.

"Do the police know who did it?" Sadie asked, her voice reminding Alissa of a bullfrog with laryngitis.

"No, not a clue," Brad mused. "They seem to think it's someone close by, though, because the person took a picture of the wreck, then left it for Alissa along with —"

Alissa placed the heel of her right sneaker

117

on Brad's left foot. "They think the person may have been watching when the wreck happened, that's all." She didn't like the idea of these two strange women knowing all the details of her personal problems. Alissa swallowed, not wanting to take time to think about her next question. "Did either of you notice anyone with a camera in the neighborhood yesterday evening around six thirty or so?"

"Now look," Sadie said bluntly and rubbed the end of her warted witch's nose. "I'm going to tell you like I told the police last night. I don't know anything about anything. Not about the bones. Not about anything else that's going on. And I don't appreciate —"

"Sadie," Mrs. Teasedale hissed. "She was just asking. You don't have to get all bent out of shape."

"I'm just trying to keep you out of trouble. She must've seen you yesterday, or she wouldn't have asked."

"Seen her doing what?" Brad and Alissa asked in unison.

Mrs. Teasedale rolled her eyes to diminish Sadies's concern. "I was just —"

"It's none of your business," Sadie interrupted, grabbing her friend's arm. "Come on, Elizabeth. Henry's waiting." And with that, the two women left, or rather escaped, the premises, leaving behind the smell of Elizabeth's lavender soap and Sadie's cigarettes.

"Strange birds," Brad whispered while he and Alissa watched through a narrow crack in the door as the women climbed into the Cadillac.

"Yeah. Did you notice Mrs. Teasedale flexing her left foot when I asked how her ankle was?"

"Uh-huh. What about it?"

"Yesterday, she acted like her right ankle was injured. You don't think . . ." Alissa suppressed a shiver.

"If Mrs. Teasedale will lie about an ankle injury, she'll lie whenever she needs to. I think they know a lot more than they told us or the police."

"About the bones, you mean?"

"About everything."

"The police officer yesterday seemed to think that the person after me was perhaps a hostile ex-patient or something." Alissa closed the door as the Cadillac drove out of view and turned to Brad.

"Maybe, maybe not." Brad stepped away from her and crossed his arms. "The reason I was going to tell them about your message yesterday was because I wanted to get their

119

reactions. I just don't trust them."

"Well, I don't either. But I didn't really want them to know all that's happening to me, either."

"Maybe they already know."

"I'd more easily believe they were involved in that bone business than in my troubles. After all, I just met them. Why would they suddenly want me — want me —" Her throat constricting, Alissa couldn't finish the words.

"Want you dead?" Brad finished, empathy softening his voice.

"Yes."

"I don't know. But I'd like to find out."

"What's that supposed to mean?"

"It means, my dear Watson, that sometimes in life we have to answer our own questions, do our own exploring." Brad thoughtfully picked up a roll of the teal and peach floral wallpaper that sat propped in the corner of Alissa's foyer. "And Sadie Horton was obviously, *very* obviously, trying to cover for Mrs. Teasedale just now. I'd like to know what she was up to when you had your wreck. I think I just might learn that a camera was involved."

"You mean that you're going to investigate them?" she asked incredulously.

"That's exactly what I mean. Wanna help?"

"Don't you think you should give the police a chance first? I mean they just started the investigation. You can't expect them to wrap it all up in one day, for Pete's sake." Alissa fumbled with the plastic wrap covering Mrs. Horton's homemade bread and gazed at Brad in worried apprehension. Everything with him was going faster than she had the nerves to stomach, and she didn't feel like "helping" him do anything. "Besides, what about all the people living across the road? How do you know they didn't do it?"

"No go. According to Richard Calbert, who, by the way, I met yesterday evening, those houses have all been built recently. So the residents are new. The forensics man said the bones have been in the ground awhile."

"But shouldn't you at least call the police before you start stirring up the neighborhood? Maybe the police are getting close." Alissa stiffened. What if the person harassing her was one of the neighbors? Would he or she become angry if Brad started nosing around, angry enough to actually kill her?

"Okay. If it will make you any happier," he said dryly, "I'll call to see if they've gotten anywhere."

She sighed and relaxed. "I think that's a good idea. Maybe the forensics lab has come up with something by now. Maybe even possible identities for the bones."

"Dream on," he said. "If you remember, they said it would be two months before they have a more exact idea of how long the bones had been there."

The phone's abrupt ringing startled Alissa into an involuntary jump. "Sorry. I'm just a bit on edge."

"Yes, and you've got every right to be. Want me to get it?"

"Would you? I'll go put up the bread; then we can go after the rental car."

"You aren't actually going to eat that, are you?" Brad asked, his hand on the white, cordless telephone located near the couch.

Alissa peered at the crusty, golden bread and remembered all the childhood fairy tales her mother had read to her about wicked witches poisoning gullible children with tainted cookies, gingerbread, or cakes. Her mother had always ended those stories with a brief, loving lecture about taking things from strangers. Had Harriett Carrington feared then that Alissa's naturally trusting nature would lead her to trouble? Alissa's heart ached with loneliness only her mother could ever fill. How she wished her mother were alive to comfort her through this turmoil.

With a shiver, she then envisioned Sadie Horton's warted witch's nose and knew exactly what her mother would advise. "I think I'll trash it," she decided.

"Wise decision." Brad picked up the receiver.

Then I'll scrub my hands, she added to herself as Brad answered the phone. Minutes later, Alissa reentered the living room, the bread safely in the garbage can, her hands red from the scrub. Brad was still talking on the phone, or rather, being talked to. Then, with an indulgent smile, he slowly recited a telephone number and hung up.

Alissa groaned. "Don't tell me —"

"Your grandmother," he said with a smirk. "She was pleasantly surprised — no, thrilled — that I'm here. So much so that she said she didn't want to disturb you; then she asked for my phone number."

"And you gave it to her?" Alissa squeaked.

"Well . . ." He shrugged. "What was I supposed to do?"

"Okay, but don't come crying to me later. You've dug your own grave."

"Oh, come on, Alissa, she can't be that bad," he teased, still toying with the roll of wallpaper he'd picked up in the foyer.

"Don't get me wrong. I love her with my whole heart. But the woman should have been an international spy instead of a homemaker. Take my word for it, before she's through, you'll hear yourself telling her what brand of toothpaste you use, what size shoes you wore in the third grade, and your college grade point average."

Brad's spontaneous laughter was the infectious kind, the kind that reminded Alissa of music, the kind that brightened a room, or someone's life. "Oh well," he said in droll resignation, his eyes sparkling. "Maybe I'll find out the same things about you."

"She'll probably tell you that, too, whether you ask or not!" Alissa sank into the wing-backed chair and shook her head, wishing for a sudden North American collapse of all phone systems. She already wanted to die of embarrassment at the prospect of what her grandmother might tell Brad. And the woman hadn't even called him yet! Before it was all over, Emily Carrington would probably detail the whole story of her relationship with Sherman Devereaux, something Alissa feared would lower Brad's opinion of her. *But what does that matter?* she asked herself, refusing to admit just how much it really did matter.

"What room are you planning to wallpaper?" Brad asked, holding up the roll of paper, his eyes still alight with laughter.

"That goes in my bedroom. You wouldn't believe the olive green and orange stuff that's in there now."

"This will be a definite improvement, then. It's a nice pattern. You know, you really have a good eye for décor." He waved his hand toward the newly decorated living room.

"Thanks. Dad would appreciate your comment. I think he was always disappointed that I didn't inherit Mom's artistic ability."

"You inherited somebody's sense of style," he said appreciatively, his gaze straying to her hair then back to her eyes.

Alissa, her pulse increasing, wondered if he was only referring to the décor of her home. The faint flame in his eyes, the same flame she'd seen at the clinic when he almost kissed her, told her he was referring to her. As their gaze lengthened, Alissa felt as if she were drowning in a pool of utter confusion. One second she wanted to avoid him, the next, she wanted to be near him.

Despite her confusion, though, she knew avoiding him would be the most practical move. She didn't want to be hurt, either, and he was obviously still very devoted to his deceased wife.

Clearing her throat, she stood and purposefully broke their gaze. "I'll put the wallpaper back in the foyer for you," she said, not knowing what else she could say as he handed her the roll.

"Need some help when you start the job? I've always enjoyed wallpapering."

"Yuck! I hate it! I've been putting it off all week, actually." Alissa didn't want to accept his offer but didn't want to appear rude by rejecting it, either. So she decided to ignore it. "Are you going to call the police before we go?" she asked, hoping he didn't suspect her reason for the subject change.

"Yeah." Was that disappointment glimmering in his eyes? Or was it his own confusion? "Where's your phonebook?"

Minutes later, Alissa sat and listened intently to Brad's probing questions and vague comments of, "Yes . . . I see . . . no, I understand . . ." His casual shrug as he hung up seemed to support his earlier assumptions about the investigation. "They don't have anything much more than they did yesterday. There were some bullets lodged in the bones, so they're convinced it was murder. But they have no leads on identification. According to the investigator, they're studying the missing persons list but haven't gotten anywhere. And of course, they have no suspects."

"Did he say anything about questioning the neighbors?" she asked, crossing her arms while trying to avoid looking at him. *Avoid his gaze at all costs,* she told herself.

"I couldn't get anything out of him other than that they gathered no conclusive leads." He thoughtfully removed his glasses. "Basically, I don't think he told me anything that we couldn't get on the evening news."

"Maybe it's because they really don't know."

"Well, I intend to find out." Brad replaced his glasses. "And I'm going to start by questioning Claire Allen. She's lived next door to Mrs. Teasedale and Mrs. Horton long enough to probably give us all kinds of information. I want to know what Mrs. Teasesdale was doing yesterday afternoon that Sadie Horton was trying to cover up."

Alissa's curiosity piqued despite herself. "Frankly, I'd like to know, too, but I still don't feel right about nosing around like that."

Brad laughed indulgently. "You didn't mind sticking your little nose over my privacy fence yesterday morning."

"I know," she said to the antique floral print hanging near her front door. "But that was different. I was still in my yard. And — and nobody had threatened me yesterday morning, either." Goosebumps broke out along her neck and shoulders, and then crept down her spine.

"I know," Brad said, taking a step toward her, only to stop. "That's part of the reason I want to question Claire. I can't let someone — someone . . ."

Alissa looked at him despite herself and saw that his floundering words were only a reflection of the turbulence in his eyes. "Besides . . ." Alissa coughed dryly and examined her broken right thumbnail. "Claire Allen raises goldfish to feed her cat. And I think that's just about as strange as anything I've seen in Mrs. Horton and Mrs. Teasedale."

"Who told you that?" His voice sounded as strained as hers felt.

"Richard Calbert. This morning he stopped by and introduced himself. He said he'd thought for years that his only normal neighbors were Mr. Jenkins and Mrs. Docker."

"Now they've moved."

"Those were his exact words."

"Oh well, raising fish for your cat isn't a crime."

"It's just odd . . . it's . . . I don't know, it's . . . different."

"Well, as far as that goes, so is Richard Calbert. He's pleasant enough, I guess, but different."

"Yeah. But he's different in a good sort of way."

"Not according to Claire Allen."

Alissa thought about the watch she'd handed him that morning, and she hoped her instincts had been right, that Claire had been wrong.

"Let's go get your rental car," Brad said, walking toward the door. "Then maybe we can go visit Claire Allen." Alissa didn't miss how he automatically included her in his visit to Claire, even though she hadn't agreed to help him. Well, he'd soon learn that she was going to be too busy.

CHAPTER 12

"Sorry to just drop by, Brad," Mr. Whit Jenkins said, pushing up his small, wire-rimmed glasses with his index finger, "but I was wondering if I could come in for a moment?"

Brad opened his front door wider so the man, who looked to be in his late sixties, could enter. He'd only briefly met Mr. Jenkins when he purchased the house, but he'd instantly liked the short, gray-haired man and his straightforward manner; perhaps because he slightly resembled Mark Twain, one of Brad's favorite authors.

"Sure. Come on in." Brad smiled his welcome, wondering what Mr. Jenkins could possibly want. Brad had returned from taking Alissa to rent a car, had eaten lunch, and was preparing for his daily swim at the YMCA. But the swim could easily wait.

Mr. Jenkins waved his gnarled oak cane around the room as he entered. "Hey, I like what you've done with the house. Nice and airy. Jan would have liked it, too, God rest her soul."

"How long has your wife been dead?"

"Ten years. Ten long years. Cancer's what took her." He walked to the nearest white leather chair and sat down, his left leg stretched stiffly in front of him. The real estate agent had informed Brad of Mr. Jenkins' car wreck three years ago, and of the resulting prosthesis which extended to his left hip.

"I bet you still miss your wife."

"Oh yeah, I think about her every day. But I was fortunate to find another woman just as good to me as she was. Took me ten years to find her, but we got married last week. That's the reason I sold the house. She sold hers, too, and we bought another one together. One that's our house."

"Congratulations," Brad said, wondering if he'd ever find anyone as special as Dana. His mind instantly conjured up Alissa's image. Alissa, peering over his backyard fence; Alissa, surrounded by her geraniums and ferns; Alissa, her brown, liquid eyes infinite pools of compassion. Was it such a crime that he was so irresistibly attracted to her?

"Mind if I smoke?" Mr. Jenkins asked, pulling a worn teak pipe and a leather tobacco pouch from his hip pocket. Brad blinked as his mind came back to the present. "No, go ahead," he said, and went to pick up Samantha from her favorite sleeping spot in the bar chair. Tobacco smoke had never affected Brad much, but it always sent Samantha into a spasm of sneezing. Ignoring her protesting yowl, Brad opened the patio door and dropped her outside.

"The reason I dropped by," Mr. Jenkins said, creating a cloud of smoke as he puffed his vanilla tobacco, "is that I wanted to look at the place where those bones were found for myself. It's mighty strange to me that I lived in this house nearly thirty years, and part of the time human bones were in the backyard, and I didn't even know it!"

Did you really not know it? Brad wondered, and then dismissed the thought. He was growing suspicious of everyone. Surely Mr. Jenkins wouldn't be involved in murder. But then, you never knew. Brad had seen pictures of mass murderers who looked even more grandfatherly and nonthreatening than Mr. Jenkins.

"You're more than welcome to take a look," Brad said, standing. "I was going to put the pool right where your rose garden was, and that's where the bones were."

"I babied those roses for years, and then you came along and just dug 'em up, eh?" he teased, his hazel eyes alight with mischief as he stood.

"Not quite," Brad said, opening the patio door. "I actually transplanted them all along the inside of the privacy fence. See?" He waved toward the backyard toward the row of multicolored roses.

"Nice," Mr. Jenkins said, admiring Brad's work. "Those roses always drove Sadie and Elizabeth crazy, just crazy." He chuckled dryly, mirthlessly. "I'd hate for them to be done away with."

"Oh?" Brad said, rubbing the nape of his neck. He'd told Alissa he wanted to question Claire Allen, but maybe his questioning would start with Mr. Jenkins.

"Oh, yeah. We had a rose rivalry that went far past friendly competition." He walked toward the hole, and Brad followed. "It wasn't my fault, really. I was content to let bygones be bygones and go on with life, but not those two."

"They are rather . . . *different,* I guess is the word."

"*Vindictive* is the word." Mr. Jenkins puffed his pipe then removed it from between his teeth as he stopped at the grave site. "Believe me, I know," he said, studying the hole. "I lived beside them many years. We're even members of the same garden club. And the year my Snowfire beat out their Tropicana for the best rose award is the year I thought they were going to put me in the ground. Did you know they actually told the police they figured I murdered those poor people, whoever they were, and buried them out here?" He pointed to the roped-off hole. "Humph. If you ask me, they did it to try to poison my roses!"

"Do you really think they might have done it?" Brad asked.

"Ah, I don't know," he placed his pipe back between his yellowed teeth and took another puff. "They're kinda mean, those two, but I don't know if they'd actually kill someone. Besides, the police don't even have the identities of the dead people. Well, yesterday they didn't, anyway. Have you heard anything new?"

"No. As of this morning, they still had no identification, and I guess until they arrive at some, the investigation stays there."

"I guess. I've heard of these kinds of things stretching on for years. At least that's the way it is on TV."

Did he sound relieved, or was it just Brad's overactive imagination? "What do you think of the other two neighbors —

Claire Allen and Richard Calbert?"

"Nicer than Elizabeth and Sadie, that's for sure. They both kinda stay to themselves, though. Always working. To tell you the truth, the only one of the whole bunch that I ever really liked was Mrs. Docker. She was like an older sister to me, especially after Jan died."

"Do you know if the police have questioned her?"

"Don't know. Haven't heard from her since she sold her house to that dentist a couple of months back. A real looker, that dentist. Never met her, but saw her coming and going some. Have you met her?" Turning from the grave site, he peered at Brad and adjusted his glasses.

"Yes, I met her yesterday." Had it only been yesterday? Why, then, did Brad feel as if he'd known her much of his life?

"You're not married, are you?"

"No. I–I'm a widower. Like you, I guess." For the first time, Brad was able to say the words without feeling as if his heart were being ripped from his chest.

"Well, it's a sad situation when you lose your mate, son. A sad situation. I spent many a night wondering why the good Lord would let Jan waste away with cancer."

"Yes, it's really bad. People just don't

know." An unspoken bond spun its way between Brad and the older man, a bond forged of loneliness and pain and confusion. For the first time, Brad felt as if someone really understood his situation, someone truly kindhearted. No, Mr. Jenkins could never have murdered two people and buried them in his backyard. If he had, then Brad's instincts were nonexistent.

"But you're mighty young still," Mr. Jenkins continued. "And that dentist is mighty good lookin'." A Santa Claus twinkle in his eyes, he winked and turned back toward the house.

The old man must be a mind reader, Brad thought as he smiled to himself. *Either that or your thoughts are completely transparent.*

Mr. Jenkins' visit stretched only minutes more. He'd obviously come simply to satisfy his curiosity, and with that done, he limped toward his nondescript blue sedan in the driveway. "Oh, by the way," he said, turning to face Brad. "I meant to ask you about your mailbox. What happened?"

"Someone accidentally hit it yesterday. No injuries." Brad instinctively glanced up and down the street, wondering if the person who cut Alissa's brake line were watching. He'd given Alissa strict instructions to call if anything else strange happened.

136

"That dentist better be careful," Mr. Jenkins muttered under his breath.

"What?" Brad asked, his brows rising in astonishment. How did Mr. Jenkins know Alissa was the one who hit his mailbox?

"Oh, um, don't forget what I said about that dentist." And with that, he hurriedly got in his car and drove away. Brad stood and watched as the blue sedan drove out of view. Had Mr. Jenkins actually suggested that he knew Alissa was the accident victim or was Brad's hearing starting to go? If Mr. Jenkins did know about her accident, then why did he ask in the first place? Could he be the one who cut the brake line?

Shaking his head, Brad shut the door. Why would Mr. Jenkins be after Alissa? They'd never even met. Apparently Brad had simply misunderstood him.

Dismissing the older man from his mind, Brad walked toward the trash can that sat near his breakfast bar. Only that morning he'd torn the sketch of Alissa into four pieces and thrown it away. But now, several hours later, Brad wanted to see it again. Fingers trembling, he removed the sketch from the wastebasket, smoothed it, and slowly lined up the ragged edges. Even though part of him wanted nothing more than to gaze at her image, another part of him still felt like a traitor, a cad.

After all, God had betrayed Dana and Kara, and Brad didn't want to likewise abandon them. But maybe there was some truth to what Alissa had said earlier. In reality, God hadn't killed them. That lunatic who pulled the trigger had killed them. Could God actually want to comfort Brad now?

"Oh, Alissa, I am so confused," he muttered. "One minute I want to pray, the next minute I don't think I can. One minute I want you in my arms, and the next I don't think I can even touch you." From the moment he'd met her, she'd affected him like a cannonball in the gut. He'd mistakenly thought his first reaction would fade, but it seemed only to strengthen, especially with someone like that Tom McDaniel practically pawing her. By her reaction, Brad didn't think Alissa cared much for Tom; or rather, he hoped she didn't care much. However, he couldn't deny that the idea of a rival had made his stomach twist in jealousy.

With a bewildered shake of his head, Brad gathered the tattered sketch and dropped it back into the trash can, a trash can he didn't plan to empty.

A smug smirk covering her face, she stroked the earth-covered gold watch with her index finger and sat on the end of her bed.

Yes, Richard Calbert had been just as much help as she'd hoped he'd be. The watch had been so easy to retrieve from that dumb Louanne Young.

Now that all incriminating evidence had been removed, she could better concentrate on killing Louanne again without worrying about the police catching up with her. She picked up the gray wig lying on her dresser and began toying with its loose curls. Only that afternoon she'd removed it from the back of her storage closet, right where it had lain for ten long years.

"Don't worry, Louanne," she crooned, picking up the silver-handled hairbrush from her dresser. "I won't do anything rash." She stroked the wig aimlessly as she stared into the mirror, into her own glazed eyes. "You ruined my life slowly, and I've decided I'll slowly ruin yours."

CHAPTER 13

"Mr. Calbert, this is Alissa Carrington, your neighbor." It was 9:30 a.m. Eight days had gone by since the attempt on Alissa's life. Alissa sat on the edge of her bed now, the telephone receiver in one hand, a roll of wallpaper in the other. She was finally going to tackle the dreaded deed, but she wanted to check with Richard about the watch she'd found first. "I'm sorry to bother you at work, but I was calling about the watch I found that you were going to take to your brother's jewelry shop. Has he finished with it?"

"Oh . . . the watch!" She heard him snap his fingers. "I completely forgot about it. I'm so glad you called. Just a minute, Alissa . . . Yes, those flowers are the ones going to Fifth Street."

Alissa listened as Richard dealt with the pressing demands of several deliveries. "Sorry 'bout that," he finally said. "It's a hectic day."

"That's okay. I understand. Listen, would it help you if I just retrieved the watch from you this evening and took it to your brother myself? I could always tell him you sent me." Although the watch wasn't an urgent matter, Alissa didn't want the situation to drag out until she had to go back to work. Then she might forget about it.

"No," he said quickly. "That's — that's okay. Like I said earlier — okay, thank you; come back, now! — sorry Alissa, one of my best customers is just leaving. Anyway, like I said earlier, my brother owes me. I'll take care of it."

"Okay," Alissa said, and with the appropriate good-byes spoken, she hung up while making a mental note to call him Monday. Alissa then stared at the atrocious olive green and orange wallpaper. The day had finally come. She'd spent the last week working in the yard, cleaning closets, shopping in Dallas with her grandmother, and avoiding Brad Ratner in general.

He'd left several phone messages for her that, after much thought, she hadn't returned. And yesterday, he'd even rung her doorbell, but Alissa hadn't answered. Her rental car was locked in the garage, so he couldn't have known that she was home.

141

Basically, Alissa was sticking by her decision to avoid him. Not that it was doing her any good. All she could think about was sun-streaked hair, smoky eyes, and broad shoulders. He filled her dreams even, dreams in which she was always in his arms.

She had to admit that she felt downright mean for giving him the cold shoulder. But wouldn't the cold shoulder now be better than breaking his heart later? She'd already gone through that with Sherman.

But Brad isn't Sherman, a little voice whispered. *Sherman wasn't a Christian. And you never felt this way about him.* True, Sherman had never caused her heart to race, nor had he created the tingles she felt only at Brad's soft touch. And if Brad ever did kiss her . . . Alissa swallowed hard, knowing she would probably melt.

When Trena had called last night to say they'd made it home safely from Corpus Christi, she'd "innocently" asked about Alissa's gorgeous new neighbor. Alissa had been as noncommittal as possible, and Trena hadn't pushed the issue.

She'd explained about her wreck as she had to her grandmother, without mentioning the failed brakes. Alissa hoped the person had gotten the thrill he or she wanted at her expense and would leave her alone now. The peace of the last week seemed to support that hope.

Before Trena had hung up, Alissa drafted her into helping with the wallpaper.

The doorbell's ring now announced that Trena was unusually punctual. Surprised, Alissa checked her sporty silver watch. "She's early, even," she muttered. For Trena, 10:00 a.m. meant sometime between ten thirty and twelve, not nine thirty.

Alissa trotted down the stairs and threw open the door, a mocking smile on her face. "So, Dr. Selver, I see for once in your life, you're on —" Her mouth fell open as she stared not at Trena, but at Brad Ratner. Brad, his hair slightly damp, his lips curled into a half smile, his left hand casually inserted in his jeans pocket.

"Expecting Trena?" he asked.

She gulped. "Yes. She's supposed to help me with my wallpaper."

"You haven't returned my calls," he said softly. "I've been worried about you. Is everything okay?" That wasn't the question his eyes asked. His eyes wanted to know why she hadn't returned his calls.

"Uh, yeah." Alissa could think of no convincing excuse for not calling him back. "I've just been . . . um . . . busy," she finally said. "Grandma and I spent the weekend in

Dallas shopping, and . . ." And what else?

"Mind if I come in?" he asked.

"No. Of course not." Alissa opened the door wide, allowing him to pass her as she closed it behind him. What could he possibly want? She thought about the first time he'd come over and they'd shared a pizza. He'd been dressed much as he was now, a crisp white shirt, a pair of worn jeans, and sneakers. He'd also looked as good as he did now. Or did he look even better today? The past week of avoiding him had left her ravenous for his company. She hadn't realized that until now. *You never felt this way about Sherman,* the same little voice of only moments ago taunted.

Alissa immediately pictured her and Brad sitting on her favorite church pew with two tiny tots between them. Somehow she knew in her gut that Brad would be an excellent husband and father, and that despite his present spiritual turmoil, he would never neglect the spiritual well-being of his children.

"Would you like a soda?" she croaked, her throat dry.

"No, thanks. I really hadn't planned to stay that long," he said, following her into the living room. "I just wanted to make sure you hadn't received any more threats." The way his gaze roamed her face, her hair, and her lips said he'd simply wanted to see her.

Alissa's lips trembled as if he'd touched them, and she clutched the back of the nearby wing-backed chair as the trembling moved to her legs. "No, thank goodness. It's been a quiet week. I was just hoping that the person, whoever it is, has decided to leave me alone. Has there been any more news on the bones?" Alissa knew the answer to that question, but didn't know what else to say. The local television station was repeatedly running spots, asking for any leads to the identity of the victims.

"No. I haven't even been able to question Claire Allen. I've been over there three times, and each time she was gone. I thought I'd try again this afternoon."

"Oh." Licking her lips, Alissa nervously ran her index finger over the mauve chair's upholstery seam and searched for something, anything, to say. But her mind was as blank as the cloudless sky. The thick tension between them didn't help her, either.

Brad rubbed the nape of his neck then nervously crammed both hands into his jeans pockets. "Alissa, we need to talk. I —"

The phone's ring stopped him in midsentence. "I bet that's Grandma," she said, her relief obvious in her voice. "She hasn't made her morning call yet." For once, Alissa hoped the older lady would talk an hour. By then, Brad would politely leave. But did Alissa really want him to leave? Seeing him felt so good, yet it was also sheer agony. Alissa could never hold him, could never feel his lips on hers. He'd made that very, very clear.

She picked up the receiver, her heart pounding out hard, even beats. "Hello."

"Alissa? Tom here. I was just calling to tell you we're finished with your car."

"Already? It's only been a week!"

"Well, I'll admit I made it top priority. Don't want my girl to be without her wheels."

She cleared her throat and decided to ignore his blatant comment. "When can I pick it up?" Tom's advances were becoming more and more possessive, and Alissa dreaded having to bluntly tell him she wasn't interested.

"Anytime today. Or, if you're free tonight, I could drive it over and we could go grab a pizza and a movie."

Her first instinct was to immediately refuse. Then she thought of Brad, who couldn't help but listen. If he thought she were dating Tom, maybe he'd leave her alone. Alissa wouldn't be in the state of

146

perpetual torment in which his presence placed her. With a quick glance his way, she turned to stare out one of the many windows lining her house's west wall and opened her mouth to accept Tom's invitation.

"No, I'm sorry, Tom," she heard herself say. "I think it would be better for me to just drop by sometime today." She simply couldn't go out with him. Not only would it be dishonest, it would also be using Tom.

"Alissa, are you ever going to go out with me?" he demanded.

She hesitated, not knowing exactly what to say, and fully aware that Brad heard her every word.

"This is me — *Tom*," he continued. "We went to the prom together, remember? Haven't you gotten over that doctor yet?"

"This has nothing to do with him," Alissa said evenly, not liking being pressured by anyone, not even a longtime friend.

"Well, why do I keep getting 'no thank you's,' then?"

"Tom, I um . . ." Alissa glanced at Brad again who now sat on the Victorian settee and scratched Frito's ear while mumbling to the dog. Maybe he wasn't listening after all. "I don't want to hurt your feelings," she said in a low voice, "but it wouldn't be fair for me to date you. You're my friend. And I can't think of you in any other way. If we were to start dating, I'm afraid you'd wind up getting hurt. Please don't be angry with me. I just can't."

"It's that Brad Ratner guy I met the other day, isn't it? I saw the way you looked at each other."

"You know I was turning you down before I met him." Alissa resisted the urge to whisper.

"Well," he continued, his voice thick, "if it's any concern of yours, you haven't kept yourself from hurting me. I really thought we could —"

"No, we can't. Tom, listen to me. There are probably women just waiting in line for you to ask them out. Am I right?" His silence answered the question well.

"I know one of them personally. She's in my Sunday school class. Carla Jamison. Do you have her number?"

Silence again.

"That's what I figured." Alissa, as always, felt like Tom's elder sister, even though they were the same age. "Now call her."

The phone's click was his answer. Smiling faintly, Alissa hung up. Tom might be irritated now, but she had no doubt he'd get over it. This wasn't the first time he'd been angry with her. That was part of the reason she couldn't take his advances seriously. Their relationship really was, and always had been, more like that of a brother and sister.

"Exactly how many men a day do you dodge?" Brad asked, a sarcastic turn to his lips.

Oh great, he was listening. "I don't keep count," she said flippantly, his remark agitating her. "Would you rather I go out with the man even though I'm not attracted to him?" Alissa dropped onto the antique couch's corner, her agitation growing to anger. Who was he to point fingers? Hadn't he been toying with her ever since they met?

"Well, exactly what type of man are you attracted to?" he asked, matching her tone. "Since you've done such an excellent job of dodging me, too, I'm curious to find out."

Obviously, Brad was more disturbed by her not returning his calls than he'd let on. But that didn't keep the tension that had been building between them since their first meeting from exploding within Alissa like a fiery volcano of confusion, frustration, and disappointment. Brad Ratner, the only man to whom she'd ever been so strongly attracted, had the nerve to sit and ask her such a question. He was the reason she couldn't sleep at night. He was the reason she couldn't eat. He was even part of the reason she'd backed out on Sherman at the last minute. Even then, before she'd ever laid eyes on Brad, she'd been waiting on him, knowing that the right Christian man was out there — and he wasn't Sherman.

"If you want to know so badly what type of a man I'm attracted to, I'll tell you." She stood on legs shaking like a toddler's, and in her present state she no longer cared about hiding the truth. "The kind of men I seem to be attracted to are men who like to play games. Men who say they want to be friends then act like they want more. You know, Brad, the sensitive, artistic type." She went on, her voice rising every second. "The type who . . . who . . ."

Brad rose from the settee and purpose-fully walked toward her.

"The type who . . ." Alissa backed away only to have him increase his speed. "Who . . ." He reminded her of a tiger, a calculating, determined, gray-eyed tiger seeking his prey. She took three more steps backward, only to run into the living room wall. "What do you think you're doing?" Alissa croaked as he placed his arms around her waist.

"I'm going to do what I've wanted to do

since the first time I saw you." His eyes narrowed to passion-filled slits as his breath fanned her cheek. "I'm going to kiss you, and do it properly."

Alissa gulped for the air that seemed to have left the room as her gaze was drawn to his mouth descending toward hers.

Tiny pinpoints of pleasure exploded through Alissa's chest, through her trembling fingers as they inched their way across Brad's shoulders to mingle in his hair. This . . . this was more than a kiss. It was a homecoming. It was what Alissa had been waiting on for years. It was right. Exactly right. And she knew now from experience what instinct had already told her. Brad Ratner was where she belonged, the one to whom she belonged.

He lifted his mouth to trail a myriad of tiny, fire-laden kisses across her left cheek and down her neck.

"Ah, Dana," he breathed.

CHAPTER 14

Alissa's spine stiffened as if she'd been struck by lightning. Brad's hands stilled in her hair. Slowly he pulled away to stare into her soul, his eyes churning, regretful.

"Alissa, I . . ."

She bit her shaking lips and blinked back the tears, not knowing which of the emotions whirling through her to express. The fury? The pain? The confusion?

Taking a deep breath, she purposed not to say something that she'd later regret. "I think you'd better leave," she finally choked out. Stepping sideways, she moved away from him. For the first time, Alissa fully realized why he'd insisted on mere friendship. A relationship with Brad would be hopeless. Not only was he still grieving his wife's death, he was still in love with her — a love Alissa now knew allowed no room for another woman.

"Alissa?"

"Just leave, Brad." Turning her back to him, she pressed her index finger between her brows. "And — and I think" — she took a quivering breath — "I think it would be best if we stayed away from each other . . . permanently."

Silence, the kind of silence that screams of high emotion, cloaked them like an icy winter's night. Brad said nothing, yet Alissa felt his gaze on her back, a gaze she couldn't bear to return. Without a word, he turned and walked out the door, softly closing it behind him.

Dashing away tears hot with sorrow, Alissa raced up the stairs to the bathroom and grabbed a box of tissues. A sob, low and mournful, wracked her body as she collapsed onto the bathtub's rim to rock back and forth like a soul lost for eternity.

She'd learned a lot in the last thirty minutes. She'd come to realize that part of the reason she'd broken up with Sherman was because she'd been waiting for Brad. At the time, she hadn't even known his name. But all the same, she'd been waiting for him. Marrying Sherman would have been more devastating than breaking their engagement. Soon after, she could have met Brad and known she'd made a terrible mistake. That would have been an unforgivable situation, much more unforgivable than what she'd opted for. She was suddenly grateful she'd prevented what would have been a disastrous marriage.

Alissa also now knew that she could love, could love with her whole being. She was certain of this because she'd made the worst mistake of all. She'd fallen in love with a man who could never return her love. The whole sad situation, so full of irony, produced a new spasm of sobs from the core of her being. Yes, Alissa knew love, knew it in its rawest, most painful form.

"Hello! Anybody home?" Trena's cheerful call rang up the stairwell. She never bothered to knock unless the door was locked.

Alissa rolled her eyes. *Great,* she thought as she grabbed a washcloth and began sponging her face in cold water.

"Alissa?" Trena called again.

"Up here!" Alissa patted her face dry with a fluffy scarlet towel, and a glance in the mirror told her the towel matched the redness of her stinging eyes. Clenching her teeth, she suppressed a new sob. Trena's arrival hadn't stopped the pain. She stepped into the hallway just as her friend, dressed in worn denim work clothes, topped the stairs.

"Ready to get to work?" Trena asked, her

new tan bearing witness of her week on the beach.

"Uh, yeah. Almost." Alissa turned toward her bedroom and hoped Trena hadn't noticed the tear seeping from the corner of her eye.

"Hey, what's wrong?" Trena placed a gentle hand on her friend's shoulder.

Alissa, wiping away the tear, squeezed her eyes shut. She wanted to tell Trena. She and Trena had always shared everything. But at the same time, the pain was so heavy, so intense, that Alissa didn't think she could bear to vocalize it. "PMS, I guess," she mumbled, walking into her bedroom.

"PMS? You've never had PMS in your life! Come on, what gives?" Trena plopped onto the end of Alissa's bed and crossed her legs, a matter-of-fact gleam in her eyes. "You ought to know by now you can't fool me. It's that man next door, isn't it?"

Picking up a bucket half full of water, Alissa didn't reply as she began sponging the old wallpaper. How did Trena always seem to know her thoughts?

"I figured something was going on last night when we talked on the phone. The minute I mentioned him, you clammed up." She tucked a strand of brunette hair behind her right ear.

155

Alissa dropped the sponge back into the water with resignation. "Okay. You're right. He's wonderful, he's a Christian, he's Mr. Right, and — and he's still in love with his dead wife," she blurted, her voice quivering.

"And you're in love with him?"

A quick nod. "Oh, Trena, I don't even know how it happened," she wailed. "I didn't mean for it to happen."

"Here, sit down. Let me have that bucket." Trena set the water bucket on the floor and drew Alissa toward where she sat on the bed and placed a supporting arm around her.

Within minutes, Alissa had told her friend the whole story, while Trena remained helplessly silent. "I never envisioned falling in love like this. I always thought it would happen slowly and painlessly."

"Not always," Trena stated flatly. "Look at Ruth and Boaz. Look at Cameron and me. I knew I was going to marry him on the second date. Sometimes it just happens that way; you just know. Besides, you know I've always said that when you really fell, you'd fall hard and fast."

The doorbell's ringing cut off any reply Alissa could form. "I'll get it," Trena said, standing. "You need to lie down for a while."

"If that's Brad again, tell him — tell him I'm in Egypt." Alissa flopped back onto the bed, wondering how her peaceful life of only weeks ago had turned into one upheaval after another.

But the upheavals weren't over. For only moments later, Trena was back at the bedroom door, her face pale despite the golden tan. "Alissa, I think you better come downstairs. There's something . . ." She swallowed hard and suppressed a shiver. "There's something you need to see."

Brad walked into his workroom, filled with the smell of fresh paint, to stare at the new portrait of Alissa that had evolved from the torn sketch. Of all the stupid things he'd ever done. Brad knew that calling Alissa "Dana" had been the most stupid. He wasn't even sure why it happened. He hadn't been thinking of her. His mind had been consumed with Alissa — her responsive lips, the smell of her jasmine perfume, and the feel of her silky hair. Even now, he couldn't get her out of his mind. Maybe he'd whispered Dana's name out of habit.

Brad studied the portrait. Alissa, on her knees near the flowerbed, her face tilted up with a ready smile, as if she were greeting someone she loved. If only that someone were Brad. He'd started and completed the painting two days ago, in what his mother called one of his "artistic frenzies." Those frenzies didn't happen often, but when they did, they usually resulted in Brad's best work. He had to admit, this qualified. Anyone who saw this painting in muted hues of blue, gray, and green would be struck by the intensity of the artist's emotion, would immediately know the subject was loved.

Despite himself, despite Dana's memory, Brad's attraction for Alissa had escalated into the beginning of a love he couldn't deny. At the same time, though, the slight guilt remained. He'd never ceased feeling married, never stopped feeling like little Kara's daddy. Even though his head told him he was free to love again, his heart hadn't forgotten his pledge of fidelity to his family.

Perhaps that was the reason he had called Alissa "Dana." His heart simply couldn't let go. So where did that leave him? A bachelor for life?

Dear God, I've never been so confused. Please help me sort out this mess. A stunned blink. Brad suddenly realized he prayed, really prayed for the first time in two years. And the peace that followed flooded his soul as if God had actually heard him. Could Alissa have been right? Could God really want to comfort him?

But how could a God who allowed innocent people to die want to comfort those left behind? Wouldn't it be easier just to prevent the deaths? That assumed, of course, as Brad had heard all his life, that God really was sovereign.

With a resigned sigh, Brad turned from Alissa's portrait to leave the room. But a quick glimpse out the window lining the north wall stopped him where he stood. Claire Allen's blue-green Pontiac cruised past, then slowed to turn toward her house.

Brad, as he'd told Alissa, had tried to catch Claire at home several times the last week. Maybe today was the day. He wanted to ask her if she'd noticed what Mrs. Teasedale was doing the evening Alissa ran into his mailbox. Sadie had obviously tried to hide her friend's actions. Brad also wanted Claire's opinion of Mr. Jenkins. His feelings toward the old man had vacillated widely during the last week. One day he was sure the kindhearted Mark Twain clone couldn't have committed murder. Then the next, Brad pondered if he'd somehow misunderstood Mr. Jenkins' comment about Alissa hitting the mailbox, or if Mr. Jenkins did indeed have prior knowledge of the accident — and perhaps much more.

Maybe Claire Allen could help him. With

one last, longing look at Alissa's portrait, Brad walked from the room.

Alissa sat up straight as a foreboding sense of doom slithered through her. The last time she'd seen Trena this pale, this stricken, was at her grandfather's funeral. "What's the matter?" she blurted.

"Someone sent you a funeral wreath, Alissa. When I first saw it, I thought it was a mistake. Then I looked at the card." She swallowed. "There's a threatening message . . ."

Her heart pounding, Alissa raced down the stairs with Trena close on her heels. She'd thought only that morning that perhaps the person harassing her had given up his or her "mission." Now she wasn't so sure.

She halted on the last stair and gazed in breathless horror at the incredibly vast spray of red roses and baby's breath. Whoever sent the thing had spared no expense. It reminded Alissa of the rows and rows of roses, which had donned her mother's grave.

"Read the message," Trena hissed from close behind as if they stood in a mortuary. Licking her lips, Alissa forced her feet to descend the last stair and walk toward the symbol of death. Arms stiff, fingers trembling, she removed the small card from its envelope. *"Alissa Carrington"* was scrawled in block letters at the top of the card. At the bottom was a note that sent her stomach into knots: *"Too bad you won't see the flowers at your nearing funeral."*

She tried to blink away the words, but they wouldn't disappear. The thinly veiled threat, she knew, was more than just a threat. Her failed brakes attested to that. Someone wanted her dead. Someone who planned to fulfill that desire.

Should she do as Brad and Tom and the policeman had suggested? Should she leave town? Even though the idea suddenly sounded appealing, Alissa knew she wouldn't run. Putting her left hand to her throat, she collapsed into a nearby chair.

"This is sick," Trena whispered, staring at the wreath as if it were straight from Rappaccini's garden of poison.

"It isn't the first time," Alissa rasped. She hadn't wanted Trena to know, hadn't wanted her to worry. But now Alissa needed to talk.

"What?" Trena shrieked, the surprise obviously jolting her from her mortuary whisper.

"My wreck . . . when I ran into Brad's mailbox. Someone had cut my brake line."

Trena's dark brown eyes widened in horror.

"Then last week, someone left a threatening message at the clinic."

This time, Trena's mouth fell open. "What did it say?" she choked out.

Alissa briefed her on the details.

"Why didn't you tell me?"

"I haven't told anyone. Oh" — she waved her hand — "Brad knows. But I didn't want to worry you."

"And your father and grandmother?"

"I didn't tell them for the same reason. Grandma would be beside herself."

"You need to call the police about the flowers."

"Why? What can they do? Advise me to leave town again?" Alissa's voice rose, and Frito, ears pricked, trotted into the living room as if he were curious about the excitement.

"It might be a good idea to go stay with your father awhile. I can take care of your patients."

"Forget it! I'm not running. How do I know this person won't resume his or her mission when I return? Or even follow me out of town?"

"You don't."

"And you know good and well you

wouldn't run either."

Trena toyed with the bottom button on her denim shirt and didn't bother to comment on Alissa's declaration. "I leave town for one week, and your life falls apart," she mused.

Alissa snorted. "Don't flatter yourself into thinking you're the glue that holds my life together." Sometimes Trena's mother-hen attitude got on Alissa's nerves.

"I was just joking." Trena rolled her eyes. "Touchy, touchy, touchy."

"Well, wouldn't you be if — if —" She waved toward the offensive wreath.

"Okay" — Trena plopped onto the couch — "you have a right to be touchy. What florist is the wreath from?" she asked, changing the subject as she was apt to do.

Alissa had been so appalled at the message that she hadn't even noticed the name of the florist.

"Maybe we could call and see if they have a record of who sent it."

"Good thinking." Alissa glanced at the card she held, but the florist's name wasn't on it. She then went to the wreath, now filling the room with a heady rose fragrance, and looked at the envelope. "I can't believe this," she gasped.

CHAPTER 15

"I was wondering if I could have a few minutes of your time, Mrs. Allen," Brad said, standing on the front porch of Claire's blue frame house. "I had a couple of questions I thought you might be able to answer."

Claire pushed her heavy auburn curls from her forehead and smiled. "Sure. Come on in. I've been out shopping this morning and have to be at the hospital in an hour, but I'll be glad to help you if I can."

Brad entered the homey living room cluttered with a neat array of knickknacks and filled with the smell of freshly brewed coffee. A twenty-gallon aquarium full of goldfish gurgled in the corner, and Brad remembered Alissa mentioning that Claire raised the fish for her cat. The lucky feline, a fat tabby, snoozed in a worn wicker rocking chair near the aquarium, his lips curled into what looked like a smug smile. By his plump appearance, Brad figured he didn't stray too far from his food source.

In seconds, Mrs. Allen had seated Brad in an outdated, brown plaid chair and handed him a mug of coffee she'd insisted he have. "Now, what was it you were wanting to ask?" she said, sitting on the edge of the couch, which matched his chair.

He politely sipped the rich liquid even though he didn't care for coffee. "I just wondered if you noticed anything, or saw anyone doing anything strange, the evening Alissa Carrington ran into my mailbox?" Brad hated to implicate Mrs. Teasedale and Mrs. Horton without first giving Claire a chance to mention them.

She thoughtfully stared at the bubbling aquarium, and Brad wondered how many hours a week she worked at the hospital. The dark circles under her eyes said she worked too long and slept too little.

"I don't recall seeing anything strange," she said, toying with the cuff of her white nurse's blouse.

Brad, clearing his throat, wondered what to ask next. He also wondered how long it would take him to starve as a private investigator. Probably about a week. "Um, did you see anyone maybe taking pictures with an automatic camera?"

"Well, now that you've mentioned it, I did. Mrs. Teasedale was in her front yard that day with a camera. I remember because I saw her when I came back home from talking with you and Dr. Carrington. I was in a hurry, though, and didn't notice what kind of a camera. Why?" Claire's thinly lined forehead creased.

"Oh, someone snapped a picture of Alissa's accident and sent it to her, and we were just trying to find out who it was." Even though his mind was whirling with what she had said, Brad tried to maintain a calm façade and casually stroked his new beard. There was no sense in getting Claire involved in problems that obviously were Elizabeth Teasedale and Sadie Horton's.

"You know, it's really none of my business, but Elizabeth and Sadie . . ." She hesitated and glanced at her hands, now clasped in her lap. "No, I'm not going to say that."

"What?" Brad set the mug of coffee on a nearby table and waited for her next comment.

"No, I really shouldn't. I felt awful the other day after I'd said what I did about Richard Calbert. He's really a nice man, and who am I to judge him?" she shrugged.

Sighing, Brad decided to go ahead and

question her about Mr. Jenkins. He probably wouldn't get anywhere, though. Claire didn't seem to be the kind who enjoyed pointing out other's faults.

"Okay. I have one other question, and then I'll let you finish getting ready for work. Did you know Mr. Whit Jenkins very well?"

"Oh, yes, a delightful man. I always thought he looked like Mark Twain." She smiled.

"Yeah, me, too. He stopped by the other day. He wanted to see where the bones were dug up. It was the first time I'd had a chance to really visit with him."

"Well, if you visit with him long, you'll notice he's a bit . . . what's the word . . . clairvoyant, I guess is the best description of him."

"Really?" Brad's interest once again peaked.

"Yes, it's strange, really. Sometimes he knows things. I've often had the odd sensation that he could read people's minds. He says it's not that, that he's just a close observer of people and their expressions."

Brad wondered if this could explain how he knew Alissa was the person who demolished his mailbox. It would also explain why he hinted that Brad should become involved with Alissa. Perhaps Brad's facial expressions were that transparent concerning the woman.

Then a new thought struck him. "If he's so clairvoyant, why didn't he know about the bones in his own backyard?"

Clair twisted the worn silver band on her right hand. "Good question. Like I said, I'm not really sure clairvoyant is the right word. He's just — oh, I don't know, he just knows things sometimes. For instance, several years ago he had the feeling that Elizabeth and Sadie were trying to sabotage his roses. They were in a stiff competition at the local garden club. Anyway, he was right, because he woke up in the middle of the night to find those two — would you believe it? — pouring water on his bushes' leaves."

Brad's blank look must have spoken his ignorance.

"You don't water rose leaves, especially not in this humid climate. It gives them powdery mildew and black leaf, which can kill them."

"Oh." He thought of the many times he'd already doused the poor roses well, thinking their leaves needed a drink just like their roots did.

"Anyway, Whit chased them out of his backyard with his shotgun at 2:00 a.m."

"A shotgun?"

"Uh-huh. You've got to understand, that's the only thing those two would understand. They're what you might call obsessive. Once they set their mind to something, no matter what it is, they're bound and determined to do it."

Brad wondered if they'd set their minds to killing those people in his backyard, or to harassing Alissa. The fact that Elizabeth had been taking pictures the very afternoon of Alissa's accident was highly suspicious, and Sadie definitely wanted to hide the fact.

But why would they bother Alissa? They barely knew her.

Claire glanced at her silver watch, and Brad took the hint. "Well, thanks for your time, Mrs. Allen, I really —"

"Please, call me Claire," she said, standing. "I'm sorry I couldn't chat with you any longer, but like I said, I've got to get to work."

"I understand." With one last look at the unsuspecting goldfish and the smiling, fat tabby, Brad stood to leave. Looked like everybody in this neighborhood had his or her odd quirks.

The envelope trembled like an extension of

169

Alissa's fingers as she stared at the florist's name.

"Who is it?" Trena asked, turning to prop her arm on the back of the Chippendale sofa.

"Calbert's Florist and Gifts," Alissa read.

"So?" Trena, brows raised, encouraged Alissa to explain her alarm.

"Richard Calbert lives just two doors down. I met him last week. He owns this flower shop."

"Are you suggesting he sent the flowers?"

"I don't know what I'm suggesting. It just shocked me. I was on the phone with him only this morning."

"Surely he wouldn't send flowers from his own shop. That would be like hanging himself."

"I know. Unless — unless —" The person who was harassing her was obviously close by, just as Richard was. Close enough to cut her brake line. Close enough to snap a picture of her wrecked car. Close enough to know she owned a gray mutt. "Unless he left his name on purpose to make himself look less guilty."

"Does he seem the type who'd harass someone?"

"No." Alissa swallowed. "He's probably not even involved. I'm sure I'm just overreacting."

"Well, let's call the flower shop and see if they have a record of who sent it."

"You call." Even though her head told her Richard Calbert couldn't be the one, at the moment she still didn't relish the idea of talking to him.

"Okay." Five minutes later, Alissa knew as much, or as little, as she'd known before Trena called. Calbert's Florist had no record of who sent the wreath. They had a record of a cash sale, but no identity of the customer. The clerk who took the money had been so busy she hadn't paid attention to the person paying the bill. And Richard Calbert had been working at his other shop when the sale was made.

"Well, at least we know it wasn't Richard himself now," Trena said, plopping back into her corner of the couch.

"I guess," Alissa said, less certain. "How do we know he didn't give someone the money to send the thing?" She sat on the edge of the sofa near Trena and stared at the card and envelope.

"We don't."

"I'm starting to feel like I should look over my shoulder every time I leave the house. I don't trust any of the neighbors anymore." The whole series of threats made Alissa want to sell her house and move to another neighborhood — the threats, plus Brad Ratner.

"Why don't we forget the wallpaper routine for today and go to the mall, then catch a movie? We can even stop and get your grandmother. That oughta liven things up and help you relax."

Alissa nodded. "That sounds good." The idea of being cooped up inside all day with her wallpaper project no longer appealed to her. "I'll change while you throw that thing away." She pointed to the wreath.

"Do you think you should call the police first, though? Even if they can't do anything, at least they'll have a record of this. You never know, it might make it easier for them to catch him."

"You've watched too many Dick Tracy movies."

"That's like the pot calling the kettle black. If I remember correctly, you're the Dick Tracy addict."

With a sarcastic smirk, Alissa walked toward the phone and once again dialed the police department's number.

The final blow. She couldn't wait to deliver it. Couldn't wait to feel Louanne's skull crack beneath the hammer. She lovingly stroked the hammer's cold metal head. Louanne's funeral would be very soon, and she'd be there in mourning, just like everyone else.

She had to seize the perfect moment, though. Louanne was probably now nervous enough to be on the alert. Well, she'd bide her time and wait, because one day, one moment, Louanne would let down her guard. Then it would be too late.

CHAPTER 16

"I hope you're happy," Sadie Horton's bullfrog voice crackled over the telephone in angry accusation.

"Excuse me?" Alissa asked breathlessly. She'd rushed into the house as she arrived from work because of the phone's shrill ringing. Alissa had thought the call would be from her grandmother, not a disgruntled Sadie Horton.

"I said, I hope you're happy!" Her voice rose to emphasize each word with staccato clarity. "The police came and questioned Elizabeth and me again! Elizabeth was so afraid they were going to arrest her, it threw her into a spell with her blood pressure, and she just came home from the hospital today! And it's all your fault!"

"What are you talking about?" Alissa narrowed her eyes.

"I'm talking about you telling the police about Elizabeth taking pictures of her flowers the day of your wreck. She had nothing to do with your wreck you little witch. I tried to tell you that two weeks ago, but you wouldn't listen!"

Alissa steadied herself and tried to remain calm. "Mrs. Horton, I didn't even know Mrs. Teasedale was taking pictures the day of my wreck." But if she had been, Alissa realized, she could have conveniently snapped a picture of Alissa's crumpled car, then left it at her clinic with that hateful message.

"Well, somebody turned her into the police!"

"I assure you it wasn't me," Alissa stated. *But if I'd known, I would have.* This was probably what Sadie had been trying to hide the day she and Elizabeth brought the bread, and it made Alissa all the more suspicious of the two women.

"I don't believe you! Ever since you and that artist moved into this neighborhood, it's been nothing but trouble. Everything was going smoothly until . . . Henry. Don't you dare," Sadie yelled. "I mean it!"

Holding the phone away from her ear, Alissa looked at it in confusion. Then the line went dead. Apparently she could thank Henry for cutting the conversation short, a conversation which left Alissa's mind whirling. Who had known of Elizabeth taking pictures and reported it to the police? Maybe Brad had somehow learned of it. Alissa reached for the phone, then stopped. She couldn't call him. Even as much as she longed to hear his soft voice, she couldn't call.

He must have been out of town the last couple of days because until last night his car had been gone. Even though Alissa had tried not to notice, her gaze still lingered longingly in his direction, as if drawn by some supernatural force.

Five days ago she'd ordered him from her life. And the crying spell Trena had witnessed hadn't been Alissa's last. Saturday morning, her grandmother had greeted her with, "Why are your eyes so red? Have you been crying?"

Alissa had shrugged off the question and changed the subject. But Grandma had been mysteriously silent about Brad from then on, and Alissa knew she suspected all was not well.

Trena had been enormously sweet and cheerful at the clinic, but it hadn't helped the heavy loneliness that seemed to penetrate Alissa's soul, a loneliness that had dulled her eyes and numbed her heart. That, coupled with the tension of not knowing who was harassing her, left Alissa emotionally drained.

Was the person perhaps Sadie Horton? She'd just now seemed angry enough to make a physical threat. Trying to shrug off the abrasive woman, she quickly changed into work clothes and consciously ignored the bedroom wallpaper, which she still hadn't replaced. Maybe tomorrow. She then grabbed a banana and headed outside. Her red and orange cannas, now blooming in the front yard, needed to be weeded. She hoped an hour of yard work would release the tension in her neck.

She'd been weeding only a few minutes, when a silver Cadillac purred into her circular driveway. Frito, sitting beside her, woofed once then promptly ignored the invader. Alissa didn't react so casually, knowing the car belonged to Sadie and Henry Horton. Had Sadie arrived to continue the accusations or to harm her physically? Alissa's mouth drying, her pulse pounding, she wondered if she should bolt into the house and lock the door. Although her thoughts were racing, her body was unresponsive, like heavy wood. She simply couldn't move. *Dear Lord, please protect me.*

The car stopped. Alissa held her breath as the skin along her spine broke out in cold gooseflesh. The Cadillac's door slowly opened, and a tall, thin, kind-faced man emerged from the driver's seat.

"Dr. Carrington?" he asked, closing the car's door.

"Yes." She swallowed, the first action other than breathing that she'd been able to produce since the car arrived.

"I'm Henry Horton." He slowly walked toward her; the anxious squint of his finely lined blue eyes suggesting regret. "I believe you were just on the phone with my wife?"

Alissa, still on her guard, stood and tightly gripped her miniature garden spade. If she needed it, at least she did have a weapon for her defense. "Yes."

"I . . ." He cleared his throat. "I just came to apologize for her behavior. Sadie sometimes gets carried away."

"It's okay," Alissa said, wondering if it really were. "I can understand why she's upset. But I promise you, I did not turn her or Mrs. Teasedale in to the police. I didn't even know Mrs. Teasedale was taking pictures the day of my accident."

"I believe you. That's the reason I came in person. You just moved into the neighborhood, and I don't want any hard feelings. Like I said, I'm sorry she even bothered you."

"Thanks." Alissa tried to smile. How did such a nice man as Henry Horton wind up with someone like Sadie?

"Well, I guess that's all I've come to say. I'll let you get back to —"

"Good afternoon," a familiar male voice said behind Alissa.

Jumping, she turned to face the reason for her sleepless nights. "You scared me," she said. Placing a hand over her heart.

He was tanner, his hair more sun-streaked than the last time she saw him. But his eyes were just as intense, just as kind as they were in her dreams, and his shoulders just as broad. His worn jeans and beige oxford shirt were still unable to camouflage his near-royal demeanor — a demeanor marked with an aggressive, protective caution.

"I don't believe we've met," Brad said, extending his hand to Henry Horton. Alissa, realizing she had been staring at Brad, made the appropriate introductions and tried to control the quiver in her voice.

All the time she wished there were a law against men being as attractive as Brad Ratner. How could she ever survive living next door to the man of her dreams, the man denied her?

"I was just leaving," Henry said, releasing Brad's hand. "But it's nice to meet you."

As the men exchanged pleasantries, Alissa noticed Richard Calbert jogging up the road. She waved in response to his friendly wave and wondered if he'd learned anything about the watch she'd found in her flowerbed. When he jogged back by on his return trip, she'd stop him and inquire.

Within minutes, Henry had driven out of Alissa's driveway to leave her standing in awkward silence with Brad and wondering why he'd come over in the first place.

"How have you been?" he asked.

"Fine. And you?"

"Fine."

She fidgeted with the hem of her stained white T-shirt. "I don't guess the police have learned anything about the bones?"

"No. They've finally given me permission to go ahead with the pool. The pool company is going to start construction again in the morning." He hesitated. "I . . . um . . . I know it's not any of my business, but what did Mr. Horton want?"

Alissa briefly told him of Sadie's phone call.

"I was the one who told the police about Elizabeth snapping pictures," he said, his gaze roaming from her eyes to her hair to her lips. "Claire Allen told me she saw her the day of your wreck."

180

"Well, Sadie Horton isn't a happy camper because of you."

"I figured as much. I'm just sorry she took it out on you. But I couldn't let that detail go by without alerting the police."

"Apparently they couldn't come up with anything incriminating, though, because they didn't arrest either woman. I mean, it's not exactly against the law to take pictures of your own flowers." Alissa's erratic pulse didn't match her calm words. She sounded as if she were carrying on a neighborly chat, when in reality a slow inferno consumed her heart. *Oh Brad, why do you have to be so unattainable?* Alissa wanted to wail the question from the highest mountaintop. Instead, she tried to avoid eye contact, a nearly impossible task, and prayed he'd leave before her traitorous body flung itself into his arms.

"I still don't trust those two. That's the reason I came over. I saw the Hortons' car, and thought . . ." He shrugged, the protective gleam still in his eyes.

"Thanks," she said to the nearby weeping willow.

"Have you had anymore threats since the note at the clinic?"

Alissa didn't want to tell him about the funeral wreath. After all, her life no longer

181

included him. Therefore, any disclosure contradicted her request that they remain apart, and mocked the intimacy they could never share.

Brad rubbed the nape of his neck. "I'm no good at this. I might as well tell you, I know about the wreath."

"How?" Alissa blurted.

He sighed. "Trena. I had a message on my machine when I got home last night. I went to visit my sister for a couple of days. Anyway, Trena's worried about you and wanted me to keep an eye on things over here."

She rolled her eyes. "Great. If it's not Grandma, it's Trena. Sometimes I think the two of them are in league against me."

"Look, Alissa, Trena has good reason to be worried. And, well . . . so do I," he added softly, his eyes gray pools of fathomless pleading. "I . . ." He stepped closer and tucked a strand of stray hair behind her ear, his hand lingering. "I've been doing a lot of thinking. That's part of the reason I went to my sister's place. I wanted to think and pray and — and talk to her."

His sporty cologne filled her senses as she closed her eyes.

"Alissa," he breathed her name in near prayerful reverence, "I missed you so much." His other arm wrapped around her waist to pull her against his chest and hold her there as if she were life's most treasured possession.

And, dropping her garden spade, Alissa couldn't resist him. Couldn't resist that overwhelming feeling that Brad's arms were where she belonged. Couldn't resist the warmth that flooded her veins. His heart, pounding out hard, rapid beats beneath her ear, matched the robust beating of her own heart. And she knew she'd died and gone to heaven . . . until his lips brushed her temple.

The feel of his lips; that's all it took. And Alissa relived that moment only days ago when he'd called her "Dana." Was he now thinking of Dana as he held her close? The thought sent an icy blast through her stomach, an icy blast that gave her the strength to push him away.

The man seemed forever determined to twist her heart into knots, and then douse her in cold disappointment. Well, Alissa wouldn't allow it to happen anymore. She was sick of his games. She'd told him to stay away from her last week, and she still meant it.

Clenching her fists, Alissa pressed her lips together with determination.

Alissa said, "Brad, I told you last week

that we should no longer see each other — period. I meant it. I'm not interested in this on-again, off-again scenario you seem intent on replaying."

"But —"

"No buts." Alissa raised her hand to stop his words, and her heart felt as if it were being wrenched from her chest. "Until you decide whatever it is you have to decide about Dana, I cannot allow you to put me through an emotional upheaval every other day."

He opened his mouth as if he were going to retort, and then snapped it shut. His jaw muscles, clenching and unclenching, were the only evidence of his anger, for his eyes were masked in cold, gray mist. "Okay," he said, a chill in his voice. "When you want to listen, call me. Until then, I'll stay out of your way, your highness." With a mock bow, he turned and stomped back to his home.

Alissa let out her breath and suppressed the tears stinging her eyes, blurring her vision. A sinking sensation in the pit of her stomach hinted that maybe she'd been too brash in dismissing him again. He said he'd been praying. Did that mean he'd finally made peace with God? But regardless of that possibility, what she said was true, and her heart, now bruised and battered, couldn't bear the thought of him calling her "Dana" again.

As Richard Calbert jogged past on his return trip, Alissa forced thoughts of Brad from her mind, thoughts she knew would soon return. "Excuse me! Richard!" she called.

Slowing, he glanced over his shoulder then came to a halt as Alissa trotted to the road. "Sorry to bother you," she croaked, trying to control her still-shaking voice. "But I was wondering if your brother has had a chance to clean and appraise that watch."

"The watch," he said in resignation, his eyes shifting from Alissa to her house. "I was afraid you were going to ask me about that before . . ." He stopped short.

"Before what?"

Richard's eyes, the eyes that only days ago had been full of a friendliness that said, "Trust me," now filled with regret. "Before I found it. I cannot believe this happened, Alissa, but I seem to have lost the watch. The other day, after you called, I planned, honest I did, to take it straight to my brother. But I couldn't find it, and I have no idea what I did with it." He raised his long, lean arms in confusion. "I've turned my house upside down, my office upside down. I don't know what happened to it!

"Look, I'm terribly sorry. I know it will turn up sooner or later, though. I'm just so absentminded lately because I've been so busy at work that I'm sure I've simply mislaid it."

"Oh," she said again, the image of the funeral wreath appearing in her mind's eye.

"Did you ever find out who sent the wreath?" he asked, as if he were reading her mind.

"Uh, no . . . no, I didn't." *Was it you?* she nearly blurted. At the same time, she wanted to turn and run. Alissa didn't know who to trust anymore. Richard had promised her he'd tend to an obviously valuable timepiece. Now the watch had conveniently disappeared. He and his staff had also denied knowing who sent the funeral wreath. Did he really not know?

"It was probably just a joke." He smiled. "One time I dressed as a minister and delivered a funeral wreath — equipped with a crazy eulogy — to someone on his fortieth birthday. One of my more memorable deliveries."

"Yes. Maybe it was just a joke," Alissa said, her voice devoid of conviction.

"Well, I've got to run. I'll let you know when I find the watch!" With a friendly wave and a ready smile, Richard jogged on toward his house.

Alissa, wondering what really happened to the expensive watch, stood near the curb until he turned into his driveway. Then she glanced toward Brad's house to see Brad watching from his living room window. Her gaze lingered with his for several breath-stopping seconds. Irresistibly drawn to him, Alissa took a hesitant step forward. Then he dropped the drapes, and she turned toward her house, her eyes blurring.

What she didn't see was Brad's expression of fervent expectation as he opened the front door. An expectation that was immediately replaced by dejected disappointment when he found no one there.

CHAPTER 17

Alissa refused to think of Brad the rest of the evening. He'd consumed her thoughts since she met him, and even the mention of his name now brought floods of conflicting emotions. Should she have remained in his arms and been grateful for the morsels of his affection? He'd seemed angry and slightly hurt that she'd pushed him away. *It might do him good,* a stubborn voice insisted. After all, Alissa wasn't any man's plaything. She was a grown woman with feelings, a woman with emotional needs that only Brad could fulfill. Now she was back to longing for his touch.

"It's best not even to think about him," she told herself as she made herself a quick chicken sandwich. Completing that task, she decided the time had come to tackle the wallpaper. The old cliché, "misery loves company," truly explained how she felt. Nothing could make her more miserable than wallpapering. So why not heap misery on top of misery and do what she dreaded most, when she felt the most miserable?

Frito wagged his tail in hopes of receiving a bit of her sandwich, and she obliged him with the last of it. "Let's go demolish that olive green stuff and put up something with some style," she said, and the loyal mutt followed her upstairs.

The first thing Alissa needed to do was change out of her trusty gardening jeans and into a pair of baggy walking shorts. At least she'd be comfortable in her misery. Opening the spacious walk-in closet, she flipped on the light and turned to face the rows of built-in shelves that lined the closet's north wall. She'd claimed this extra space for her shorts, sweaters, and jeans stowaway shortly after moving in.

A quick scan of the shelves didn't produce the particular pair of shorts she was searching for, though — the khaki ones that she'd bought last summer. They were too big when she bought them, and that's the reason she liked them so much. Big equaled comfortable. Finally, after moving two pairs of blue jeans, she found them crammed into the left corner of the second shelf.

Alissa grabbed them and started to turn from the closet, when something caught her eye. A piece of folded paper, yellowed with age, was wedged into the shelf's far corner. Her curiosity heightened, she reached for the paper to unfold it and read the message scrawled in masculine script.

Louanne,
    I've finally told her. Our plane for Australia leaves tonight. Be ready by eight.

All My Love,
Richard

Alissa blinked. The only Richard she knew nearby was Richard Calbert. Why would a note he'd written be in Mrs. Docker's house, and who was this woman named Louanne? It didn't take a brain surgeon to figure out the note was setting up a lovers' rendezvous.

Louanne. The name for some reason sounded familiar. She was sure she'd heard it mentioned since moving to this neighborhood. But when, and by whom? Nibbling her thumbnail, she wondered if Mrs. Docker would know.

Normally, Alissa would have shrugged off such a note as the leftovers of the house's last owner and trashed it. But the fact that Richard's name was at the bottom fanned her curiosity's flickering flame into a roaring inferno. Richard Calbert seemed too entwined with the strange things happening to her. Perhaps an explanation of this note might further reveal his true character.

She grabbed the phone book from her nightstand, looked up Mrs. Docker's number and dialed it, only to receive a recording. After leaving a brief message, Alissa hung up and stared in determination at the wallpaper.

Brad sat in his living room, deep in thought. He'd suspected he'd blown his chance at a relationship with Alissa when he called her "Dana." Now he knew he had. His sister had simply shaken her head when he told her the whole story.

"You've just fouled up in the worst way possible," she'd declared. "You'll be lucky if she ever speaks to you again."

Even apart from the good counsel of his sister and time spent with his brother-in-law and nephew, the visit to their east Texas farm had done Brad a lot of good. He'd been able to do some soul-searching and, yes, to bring some closure to the healing process begun when he lost his family. That meant realizing he couldn't blame God for what happened. He still didn't understand why God hadn't prevented his wife's and daughter's needless deaths, and he probably wouldn't understand. But it was time to accept what had happened as he accepted God's comfort.

Alissa's words had brought him to this realization, a realization his sister had confirmed. Yes, Brad had finally resolved his anger toward God and asked forgiveness for it, and now felt a peace within he hadn't experienced since before the fateful day he'd entered that fast-food restaurant with his family. Now he knew he had to create a new life for himself.

These decisions had led to the painting that he now inspected — a dilapidated log cabin nestled at the base of wooded hills. Only weeks ago, he'd wondered what he would do to keep the art galleries happy when his old paintings were gone. Now he no longer had that worry. For that driving urge, that undeniable force which bade him to paint had returned with a new intensity.

Alissa. He could thank her for reawakening him emotionally and spiritually as man and artist. The irony of the whole situation was that he'd pushed her so far away, he didn't know if he could ever reach her again.

Brad rubbed the nape of his neck and stared out on the patio doors. Grinding his teeth together, he made an irreversible decision. First, he'd give Alissa time to cool down. Then he'd kill her with kindness, slowly wear down her defenses, and not take "no" for an answer.

Along with his emotional and spiritual healing, the trip to his sister's home had also resulted in a vague toothache in one of his left, upper molars. With a calculating smirk, Brad decided he should have a dentist examine his teeth immediately.

Two evenings lapsed before Alissa heard from Mrs. Docker, evenings in which Alissa had finally replaced the old wallpaper with the new. Staring at her accomplishment with satisfaction, she picked up the ringing phone in her bedroom and heard Mrs. Docker's kind soprano voice on the line.

"I called the other day," Alissa said, "because I found an old note in my closet, and was wondering if you might recognize it." She picked up the note she'd left lying beside the telephone and read it.

"Mmm . . . that doesn't sound familiar," Mrs. Docker said. "The only Richard nearby is Richard Calbert."

"That's what I thought."

"And I don't know anyone named Louanne."

Come on, think, Alissa urged. For some inexplicable reason, learning about the note had become of monumental importance to her. She knew she'd heard someone mention the name "Louanne" recently. If she could only remember who and when, she felt as if . . . she didn't exactly know what she felt. It was one of those sixth-sense sensations that her grandmother said Alissa shared with her mother.

"Let me think on it a few days, and I'll let you know if I come up with anything. It seems like I should know something, but my memory's not like it used to be, especially not since my heart attack last fall."

The real estate agent had explained that it was due to failing health that Mrs. Docker had wanted to sell her house and move into a retirement home. She now had a private apartment in assisted-living quarters where she had easy access to a nearby hospital.

"Okay," Alissa said. "Call me anytime. Do you have my number at the clinic?"

"No."

She slowly recited the number, then, after exchanging pleasantries, hung up. Maybe the older woman would have a memory flash tomorrow.

Tomorrow. Alissa thought about coming down with a convenient case of the black plague when she thought of her appointments for the next morning. Brad Ratner was first in line. The receptionist said he'd called early yesterday morning about a toothache and insisted that Alissa, not Trena, should see him.

Alissa didn't know what to think of this turn of events. The truth was, one second she wanted to avoid the appointment, while the next, she couldn't wait. Her head and her hurt pride told her to skip the country for a day, while her heart told her to enjoy every second of his presence.

The next morning as she entered her office, her feelings were still vacillating between dread and happy expectation.

"Who's your first appointment? A regular?" Trena asked, entering to give Alissa her morning cup of coffee while Alissa ate her usual breakfast banana.

"No. A new patient," she said as noncommittally as possible and dropped the banana peel into the trash can beside her desk.

"I've got the Wilson kid." Trena rolled her eyes and sat on the edge of Alissa's desk. "Don't be surprised if we get serenaded by a chorus of screams."

"Dr. Carrington?" Molly Langford, their middle-aged, plump dental assistant, peered into the office. "Mr. Ratner is here. It's early, but I thought you might want to go ahead and get started, so I put him in the first chair."

Alissa swallowed and grabbed a breath mint from her drawer. "Thanks."

"Brad Ratner?" Trena whispered.

"Yeah."

"He's your first appointment?"

"Yeah. He says he has a toothache."

"Either that or a heartache," Trena said with a smug snicker and left for her own office.

Grimacing at her friend's back, Alissa straightened her freshly starched lab coat then headed for the inevitable.

She'd waited long enough, and Louanne could live no longer. Tonight, the moon would be full, just like it had been ten years earlier. The perfect time for a murder.

"You should have been more careful, you double-crossing witch," she said to her reflection, and stroked the dull gray wig now resting on her head. "This time, I'll make sure you don't escape from your grave." With satisfaction, she picked up the nearby hammer and slammed it against the bathroom mirror, enjoying the vibration reaching to her elbow — the same vibration she'd feel when the hammer smashed Louanne's skull.

Chapter 18

Alissa walked briskly into the examination room, her spine stiff. "I understand you've got a toothache," she said in her most businesslike voice, a voice that hid the fluttering of her heart. Sitting down on a nearby stool, she looked Brad squarely in the eyes and attempted to act as if nothing had ever passed between them.

"Yeah. It's on the top left," Brad said, his eyes seeming to recount the moment they'd shared that blazing kiss. "I can't really tell which tooth it is. It's either the third or fourth one back."

She willed her face to remain impassive. "That's fairly common. When was the last time you had your teeth cleaned?"

"Three months ago." He looked as if he'd just told her he loved her.

"No cavities then?" she squeaked as Molly handed her a mirror.

"None."

"Have you eaten anything hard the last few days?"

"No."

His voice was as soft, as caressing, as hers was businesslike in the extreme. And Alissa wondered why he'd really come in. There were many other dentists he could have seen.

"Okay." She stood and covered her mouth and nose with a blue examination mask. "Let me have a look, and then we'll take some X-rays."

He opened his mouth obediently, his gaze never leaving her face. She purposefully concentrated on his molars as she examined them with the mirror and tried to still her trembling fingers. "Does that hurt?" she asked, pressing against his tooth with the explorer Molly supplied.

"Uh-uh."

"Okay, let's take some X-rays and see what we can find out." The dental assistant silently tended to the X-rays as Alissa left the room to check the time of her next appointment and regain her equilibrium. Minutes later she reentered, expecting to find Molly with the processed X-rays. Instead, she found Brad still alone. Alissa prepared to bolt back into the hallway. But

Brad grabbed her hand before she could escape.

"Alissa, I'm terrible at this," he said.

"At what?" she croaked and tried to pull her fingers from his grasp, but he only tightened his hold.

"I do have a toothache, but I don't even care about that right now," he declared, and his little-boy smile made the room spin.

She stared at him in silence. "Then why did you —"

"I made the appointment because I just wanted to see you."

"You what?" Her voice rose in pitch, partly in professional incredulity, partly in feminine pleasure. "You could have . . ." She lowered her voice to a whisper. No sense in Trena and Molly and any waiting patients overhearing their conversation. "You could have walked about forty yards from your front door and done that."

"Yeah, if you chose to answer the knock at your door."

Alissa gritted her teeth as new irritation replaced the original pleasure. He was still up to his little games. Now he wanted to see her. By three o'clock he would probably barely speak to her, and more than likely he was thinking of Dana at this very minute. The very memory of his calling her Dana sent Alissa into a fit of fury. "Look, if you don't want me to find the cause of your toothache, then I have a schedule to maintain." She pulled her hand from his.

"Hey, I'm paying for your time." He stood and ripped the blue plastic bib from around his neck.

"Well, what did you want to see me for?" she whispered, her fists tight wads of tension.

"I just wanted to see you," he whispered, placing hands on her shoulders.

"Okay, you've seen me. Now go." She backed away from his touch. "I've already told you twice, and I guess I'll have to tell you again —"

"Look, I'm sorry for calling you 'Dana.' It was a mistake, a really unfortunate mistake."

"A mistake?" Alissa raised her brows. "No, I think you just spoke the name of the person on your mind, and it wasn't me!"

Brad stepped toward her, decreasing the number of feet between them to inches. "I think more than anything else, your pride is what's hurting," he said, his voice sounding relieved, his eyes sparkling with humor.

"Pride!" she hissed, backing closer to the room's corner. The nerve of the man! "Since when did you grow into such a mind reader? Besides, what if it is pride! How would you like it if I called you . . ." She started to say Sherman, then stopped herself.

"Sherman, you mean?" He once again narrowed the space between them.

"How do you know about him? No — don't answer that. I know how you know. My grandmother, right?"

"Bingo." Brad reached for her hand, but Alissa deftly sidestepped to cross the room.

"Look, we're getting nowhere with this, and I have patients coming, so why don't you just —"

"I don't care if she is with a patient!" a familiar female voice yelled from the hallway. "She's my granddaughter, and I need to talk to her. Now let me pass right now!"

"Oh, no," Alissa groaned and stepped into the hall to see Molly trying to corral Emily Carrington back toward the waiting room.

"Mrs. Carrington," Molly urged, "Dr. Carrington will be with you in just a few minutes. I promise. If you'll just wait —"

"There you are," Emily said, pointing to Alissa. "Tell this pit bull of yours to let me pass!"

"It's okay, Molly," Alissa said, crossing her arms.

With a smirk, Trena walked by, heading for the back examination room. "Having an eventful morning aren't we?" she mumbled.

"Just wait, you're next. And I'll be the one grinning when the Wilson kid gets here."

"I need a ride home, Alissa," Emily said, walking toward her granddaughter, determination glimmering in her clear blue eyes. "Can you take me?"

"Grandma, couldn't you call a taxi?"

"You know I hate taxis."

"Well, how did you get here in the first place?"

"Hello, Brad," Emily said.

Alissa glanced behind her to see Brad smiling indulgently.

"Hello, Emily," he said politely.

"I'll tell you how I got here." Emily continued, as if she'd not spoken to Brad. "That Samuel Reynolds talked me into letting him drive me to the drugstore. You know, the one across the street that gives the senior citizen discounts. Anyway, he got me in that parking lot in his red Corvette with its tinted windows, and do you know what he had the audacity to do?" She tugged on the lapel of her Chanel jacket, her expression one of near horror. "He put his hand on my knee and tried to kiss me, that's what!"

Alissa, biting her bottom lip to stop the smile, heard Brad's barely stifled snicker.

"So I told him, I just said, 'Samuel Reynolds, I never kissed but one man in my life and that was my husband.' " She shook her finger at Alissa's nose for effect. " 'And if you think I'm going to start kissing men now, you're crazy!' That's just what I told him." Emily placed her hands on her hips in an indignant pose. "I've watched the evening news, and I know! You can get *germs* from kissing men!"

Staring at the toes of her penny loafers, Alissa pressed her lips together until they hurt. "Well, did you get what you needed at the drugstore?" she managed to choke out.

"No! I never went in! And now I can't even remember what I went there for! That's why I just want to go home!"

"I can give you a lift," Brad said. "I was about to leave anyway."

"Oh, could you?" Emily pleaded. "That would be so kind." She looked at Alissa. "He's a lot nicer than that Sherman character. I'll never know what you saw in him."

"We aren't through with our conversation," Brad muttered as he passed Alissa.

"As far as I'm concerned we are," she whispered, raising her chin in defiant determination. "Until you decide you're ready for a normal relationship —"

"Who says I'm not?" he challenged.

Alissa stared at him, not knowing exactly what to say. If Brad really were ready for a relationship, then that changed the whole picture. The question was: Could she trust him?

"Are you coming, Brad?" Emily called from down the hallway.

"Yes." He stroked Alissa's cheek with the back of his index finger, leaving a trail of tingles behind. "We'll talk tonight, okay?"

Swallowing, she hesitated. If she agreed, she might be stepping right back into his emotional hurricane. But if she turned him down, she just might be turning down the very man God had chosen for her.

Brad's eyes darkened in anxiety as the silence stretched between them and Alissa continued to deliberate.

"Okay," she finally said, and hoped she hadn't made a mistake.

His face relaxed. "Okay, then." And with a slow wink, he turned to leave.

CHAPTER 19

Brad knocked on Alissa's front door and waited, but no answer came. He glanced at his watch, six o'clock. Perhaps he was rushing in his eagerness to talk with her. He'd gotten her to agree to listen to him more easily than he'd expected to. Now if he could just convince her that he truly cared for her.

Knocking again, he tried to suppress the tiny fear that tugged at him. Alissa usually arrived home by now. *She probably had to stop at the grocery store or something,* he thought. Her Mustang wasn't in the driveway, so Brad walked to the closed garage. He hopped several times in an attempt to peer through the garage windows. Finally, he saw that the garage was empty.

The tiny fear slowly grew into stark apprehension. Brad couldn't explain it. The feeling was like some ominous, dark cloud that steadily descended on him and purposefully penetrated his soul. Perhaps he should go to the clinic just to make sure she hadn't had car trouble.

Turning from the door, he hoped car trouble was the only problem she'd experienced. After all, someone had already tried to kill her, and the funeral wreath promised another attempt. Maybe that was the reason for Brad's anxiety. But wasn't that reason enough?

With determination, he rushed to his Lexus. Something told him all was not well with Alissa. Something he could not ignore. He raced to his vehicle, whipped his cell phone from his belt clip, and retrieved the phone book he kept beneath the front seat.

She opened the storage closet's door an inch and peered into the clinic's empty hallway. The only person now at the clinic should be Louanne. She'd heard her tell her partner she was going to stay an extra hour to clean her office. The light from her office attested to that.

After warily listening for several seconds, she felt confident that, except for Louanne, the clinic was indeed empty. With a gentle push on the door, she stepped into the hallway and silently unlocked the back door, opening it only an inch. This would be means for escape after the murder.

She'd been waiting one hour for the staff to leave. Sneaking in at five o'clock had been so easy. She'd simply walked into the empty waiting room as if she belonged there, slipped by a distracted receptionist, and then crept into the storage closet. The rest had been a matter of waiting until the last "good-bye" was said. Louanne had told the receptionist to lock the doors as she left for the night.

She smiled. The doors were locked, but Louanne was trapped with a murderer.

Now the fun will begin. She lovingly caressed the hammer in her right hand and relived the moment she smashed her bathroom mirror. She couldn't wait to do the same to Louanne. Licking her lips like a predator, she continued her trek down the hallway. Like a prowling panther, she stopped just outside the office doorway and watched as Louanne, her back turned, inserted several books into their proper places on the floor-to-ceiling bookcase behind her desk. Louanne always did enjoy books. Too bad for her she didn't stick to reading them.

Her right eye nervously twitching, she adjusted the gray wig, raised the hammer, and approached her prey.

Alissa ignored the ringing phone. She never answered the phone when she stayed after hours, and she wasn't about to start now.

She placed the next to last book in the bookshelf. Alissa was notorious for removing books then forgetting to replace them. And her forgetfulness had created a growing stack she could no longer ignore. She'd also decided to straighten her office before going home.

Home. Where Brad waited next door to speak with her. Alissa wondered exactly what he would tell her. That he loved her, perhaps? As much as she longed to hear the words, she still had nagging doubts about their sincerity. Could he have gotten over his wife already, when only weeks ago he was still so obviously devoted to her memory?

These questions filling her thoughts, Alissa bent to retrieve the last book.

She took another step, hovering behind Louanne and trying to decide whether to immediately slam the hammer into her head or call out her name. Wouldn't it be a terrible shock for Louanne to once more face her murderer? It would be terrible for Louanne, entertaining for her. Savoring the powerful moment, she finally decided to strike from behind and do it quickly. The longer she waited, the more likely she was to get caught. Besides, Louanne had been so naughty, she'd immediately know who hit her.

Brad tried the knob on the clinic's door only to find it locked. "Good girl," he muttered. Relaxing, he took in the smell of summer pines and eyed her Mustang in the parking lot. The top was up and the doors appeared to be locked. Alissa was obviously taking no chances. His relief increasing, he pounded on the door with a force that ensured she'd hear him. "Alissa? It's me, Brad. Are you in there?"

She lunged for Louanne, who, in response to Brad's call, stepped away from the desk just in time to miss the brunt of the blow. Her stomach tightening, she watched as Louanne sank to her knees after receiving the glancing blow behind her right ear. With the hammer heavy in her sweaty hand, she stood over her victim like a conquering mountain lion that has maimed an innocent sheep and prepares to make its fatal move.

"Alissa?" Brad's call increased in urgency as he continued to knock.

After a nervous glance down the hall, she wondered if she should complete her mission or run? Did she have time? With the front door knob rattling, the murderer decided to make her escape. She would be forced to finish Louanne's punishment later, perhaps tomorrow.

She then raced for the back door to move stealthily outside and run toward her car, parked two blocks away.

Now frantic, Brad backed away from the clinic's doorway, took two purposeful steps forward, and rammed his sneaker into the door just below the knob. It popped open with a splintering protest.

"Alissa?" he called again, fearing what he might hear and at the same time fearing the silence. Brad rushed through the waiting room to see a light down the hall. "Alissa?" His heart pounding in his temples, he ran toward the ajar office door. What he found wrenched his soul.

His worse nightmare, he was reliving it all again, Dana, dead at his feet. But this time it was Alissa. Her body sprawled beside the desk. Her pale hair splayed across her equally pale cheek, a trickle of blood oozing from behind her right ear.

Brad couldn't move, couldn't breath, he couldn't blink. Was he forever destined to fall in love, only for it to end in death?

Her eyelids fluttering, Alissa groaned and slowly reached to touch the back of her head.

"Alissa," Brad croaked. Rushing forward, he knelt beside her to stroke her cheek. "Alissa, can you hear me?"

"Brad?" Another groan. This time, her eyes opened. "Someone st–struck me from behind. My head." She tried to roll onto her back.

"No, no, don't move." He didn't have extensive medical knowledge, but knew enough from college football to understand her need to lie still. "I'll call an ambulance."

"I — I think I'm okay."

He gripped her hand and gently kissed her cheek. "You're not okay until they say you're okay. Now don't move," he commanded.

"You're going to be fine," the young physician said two hours later. "There are no signs of concussion, and the CAT scan looks fine." He went on to give her instructions for overnight observation.

Sighing, Alissa sat up on the edge of the

emergency room examination table on which she had been lying.

"Do you feel like talking to the police?" Brad asked, pointing toward the middle-aged cop hovering near the waiting area.

"Yes." She gingerly fingered the small cut two inches behind and above her right ear. The only pain she suffered after the wound cleaning was soreness to the touch and a headache.

"You were very fortunate," the police officer said minutes later as Alissa, Brad, and he chose seats in the emergency room waiting area.

"That's what I keep thinking." She instinctively grasped Brad's hand as it closed over hers. He'd ridden with her in the ambulance, and she'd been grateful for his presence, was still grateful for his presence. He was like a rock, quiet and solid, exactly what she'd needed in her time of terror.

The dark-skinned policeman, whose nametag read R. BLACKFOOT, wasted no time in his questioning. "Can you recount exactly what happened?"

Alissa glanced at Brad. "I was in my office, reshelving some books, when I heard Brad's knock on the clinic's front door."

"I take it the door was locked?"

"Yes. As I turned, I felt the blow — like

something hard, maybe metal."

"Did you see the assailant?"

"No. I blacked out immediately — wait a minute. I did catch a glimpse of curly, gray hair."

The officer, scribbling in his notepad, never looked up. "Short or long? Male or female?"

Alissa blinked. "Well, it was rather fluffy, I think." She shut her eyes and tried to reconstruct what she had seen in a mere glance. "I don't know. I guess it looked more like a woman's hair, but it's hard for me to say. Then, the next thing I knew, Brad was telling me to lie still."

"It's a good thing you were there," Blackfoot said, glancing at Brad.

"A very good thing," Alissa added. Squeezing his hand, she smiled her appreciation into eyes that smiled back and held the glimmer of unrestrained affection.

The officer discreetly cleared his throat. "I'm going to have to take a look at your office. Do you feel like driving over there and letting me in?"

"Alissa, are . . . are you all right?" Trena, her dark eyes full of panic, rushed through the waiting area doorway and straight for her best friend.

"I'm fine," Alissa assured her.

"I wasn't home when Brad called." She knelt in front of Alissa to anxiously peer into her face. "He left a message on my machine, and I hit the ceiling."

"Just calm down. I'm going to be fine."

"Wait a minute! I'm supposed to be the one to tell you that."

"Yeah, but I'm not as high-strung as you are."

"What happened?"

Alissa quickly briefed her friend.

"I knew it! I had a strange feeling about leaving you at the clinic by yourself!"

"But I made sure the doors were locked. I don't know how the person got in."

"That's what we want to try and find out," Officer Blackfoot said.

"Could you let him into the clinic, Trena?" Brad asked. "I'd really like to get Alissa home."

"I'd like very much to go home," Alissa said. All she wanted was a long hot bath and a cup of even hotter tea. Facing the clinic right now held no appeal for her.

"Sure," Trena said. "I'll do anything to help. And just for the record" — she shook her finger at Alissa's nose — "I'm spending the night at your house tonight."

"No, I am," Brad stated emphatically. "I plan to camp out on her couch. That way, if anyone tries to break in, they'll have to get past me before they make it to the stairway. Besides, the doctor wants someone with her overnight. She's supposed to say up awhile then be awakened every few hours."

"Thanks," Alissa said, secretly glad for the protection.

"I think that's a good idea," Blackfoot said. "I wish we had enough manpower to have someone sit outside your house tonight. As it is, the best we can offer is a regular patrol of the neighborhood. But rest assured, we'll be watching."

"Good," Alissa said, wondering if she were safe anywhere. Somehow the intruder had noiselessly entered the clinic. *Could the same person be waiting for me at home?*

CHAPTER 20

"I've looked through every closet and your attic," Brad said an hour later. "So unless this sicko is invisible, we're here alone."

Alissa sighed in relief. After a thorough search of the house's first floor, Brad had gone upstairs, and Alissa had sat with her gaze riveted on the stairwell. She'd never felt so vulnerable in her life, and hoped her assailant would be caught before it was too late. Who did she know with gray hair? That one clue obviously did not lead to Sadie Horton or Elizabeth Teasedale. Perhaps the two women were simply bored and nosy and not in the least bit connected with Alissa's problems of late.

"I'm sure that monster would have killed me if it weren't for you," she said, wrapping her arms around her midsection in an attempt to feel more secure. "I never did get around to thanking you." A smile wobbled its way along her lips.

"That's what we knights in shining armor are for, ma'am." Brad, delivering another of his exquisite smiles, sat beside her on the Victorian settee and placed his left arm across her shoulders.

Alissa instinctively snuggled closer, loving the strength that arm represented, loving his masculine scent and, yes, loving him. Right now, she didn't care who he was thinking about. Alissa simply needed his touch.

"We knights are also available for hugging." He leaned forward to place his right arm on her waist, pulling her closer. His eyes, only inches from hers, beckoned her to respond to his embrace, an invitation totally unnecessary.

Alissa's heart palpitated in anticipation. Her breath, shallow and short, steadily increased in pace. And her skin tingled everywhere he touched her — her shoulders, her waist, and now her cheek as he gently stroked it with his thumb.

"And for kissing," he whispered against her lips.

Their previous kiss paled in comparison to the one that ensued. Alissa, wrapping her arms tightly about his midsection, responded with an abandonment which blocked out their conflict and filled her

218

senses with Brad and Brad alone.

The kiss finally ended, only to have Brad pull her closer and desperately whisper in her ear, "Ah, Alissa, I'm so sorry. I feel like I've messed everything up between us. I — I know I've acted like a confused teenager, but can we just start again?"

Her throat dry, Alissa placed her head against his shoulder and reveled in the sensation of his warm breath on her ear. Right now, she'd agree to being burned at the stake with him. But a voice of caution whispered in the back of her mind. *How do you know he really means it? Tonight he calls you Alissa but what about tomorrow? Will it be Dana again?*

As much as she wanted to say "yes" to his request and ask no questions, Alissa knew she had to express her fears. They couldn't start over without completely clearing their past. Reluctantly, she forced herself to pull away from him and look into his pleading eyes. "There's nothing I would like more than our starting over, Brad. But I think we need to talk first, don't you?"

"Yes. I — I guess I'm rushing things, aren't I? Sorry." He wrapped a strand of her hair around his index finger.

"It just seems a little — I don't know — quick for you to want a relationship with me when only weeks ago you were calling me Dana." There. She'd said it. And even though she felt ungrateful for having voiced her opinion in the face of his honest admiration, Alissa felt better for having done it.

"It really hasn't been quick, you know. It's taken me two years to get over her." He stared across the room at Frito, who snoozed on the bottom stair. "What happened, I think, was that I met you at the very end of my grieving. Either that or meeting you shocked me out of it." He chuckled. "In the words of Whit Jenkins, you're 'quite a looker,' Dr. Carrington. And if you want the truth, I haven't been able to think straight since I saw you peering over my backyard fence." Brad, shrugging, toyed with the button on his blue cotton shirt. "I've just had some problems dealing with feelings of betrayal to Dana and Kara. See, just because they died, I didn't stop feeling like a husband and father."

"And what about God?" Alissa asked, hating to push the issue, but at the same time, needing an answer. "Where does He fit into all this?" As much as Alissa cared for Brad, she needed to hear him say that his relationship with the Lord was once again stable. Even though her heart told her he wouldn't shirk his family responsibility as a biblical

220

husband, she still needed to hear his confirmation. She'd learned her lesson and learned it well, with Sherman.

"You were right, Alissa. God didn't kill my family. He allowed the tragedy, though. I don't understand why —"

"And you probably never will. There still are times when I wonder why He allowed my mother to die while she was still so young."

"I guess we're a couple of people who have lost a lot. But I also know we're a couple of people who God cares a great deal for. That's what I've come to realize all over again, that even though I was shaking my fist at God, He still loved me. I'm not saying I've 'arrived' spiritually. I still have a long way to go. But at least I know, and He knows, I'm back to giving it my best shot."

Relieved by his words, Alissa laid her head on Brad's chest. Yes, this was the man God had prepared for her. "That's what's so amazing about Him. He never gives up on us. I know it had to have been pure misery — what you've been through. Seeing my mother die was bad enough, but I can't imagine seeing her slaughtered. Do you know that even though it's been fifteen years, I still miss her? Sometimes I'm still tempted to get angry."

"I'm sure that's a temptation I'll have to overcome myself. But at the same time, I can't keep living in the past. I don't think Dana or Kara either one would want that. I've got a future to think about."

She pulled away to look into his eyes. "I don't expect you to forget about them, Brad. That would be inhuman. It's just —"

"I know. I'll never forget them. I loved them both with my whole heart, and a part of me always will. But I've still got to live today. I've got my painting . . . and you, I hope."

His last statement, so full of uncertainty, sounded more like a question, a question that melted all of Alissa's remaining reservations. For this time, she knew he meant it. "Yes, you've got me," she whispered, sealing her promise with a kiss.

Alissa awoke the next morning to the smell of frying bacon and freshly brewed coffee. Stretching lazily, she smiled and reflected on the previous evening of promises made. Brad hadn't proposed, of course. They hadn't known each other long enough for that.

But the pledge was in his eyes, so full of love. Alissa would be content for now in the "getting to know each other" stage of their new relationship. And when Brad did ask, she'd answer with a resounding "yes." Chuckling, she thought of her father's shock when he would learn one day that Brad Ratner was going to be his son-in-law.

She arose, quickly showered and dressed, then headed down the stairs with Frito on her heels.

"Hey, sleepyhead," Brad said, greeting her with a ready smile and a soft kiss on her forehead. His hair, mussed from sleep, his shirt outside his jeans, his eyes, still drowsy — all this made Alissa look forward to the day she'd greet him every morning.

"It's early," she said, glancing at the kitchen clock that said six thirty. Too bad they couldn't spend the day together.

"Yeah, well, I didn't exactly have a king-sized bed last night."

"Was it too terribly uncomfortable?"

He shrugged. "Not too bad. But even if it had been a bed of nails, I'd have slept there. I'm still worried about you and this lunatic."

"You aren't the only one." Alissa caressed the scabbed-over wound in her hair as she recalled the three nightmares from which she had been awakened. "Thanks for checking on me during the night." Brad had followed the doctor's orders and awakened Alissa every three hours to make sure her slight head injury hadn't developed into something more serious.

"Anytime," he said as if he meant it. "Want some coffee? I made it just for you. I'm not a coffee person."

"Sure."

"Do you feel like going to work?"

"Yeah. My head's not hurting, so I don't see why I shouldn't be able to."

"Well, in that case, I thought I'd go home and shower then come back to drive you in. Would you mind?" He took a blue mug from the cabinet, filled it with the aromatic coffee, and handed it to her.

"That would be great." Delighted at how comfortable Brad appeared in her kitchen, Alissa took the mug. "To tell you the truth, I don't relish the idea of driving anywhere alone."

Trena had called at nine o'clock the night before with news that the investigating officer hadn't found anything incriminating at the office. This hadn't surprised Alissa. Whoever was harassing her was adept at covering his or her trail.

"What time do you usually leave?"

"About eight."

"Okay. I'll be back at about a quarter till, then. I left enough bacon and eggs for you." He pointed to the stovetop.

"Thanks. This could get to be a habit." She smiled her most flirtatious smile and knew Trena would be proud.

"Who knows, it just might." With a playful tweak of her nose, he planted a kiss on her mouth, which pledged it *would* become a habit. "Lock the door behind me," he said as their embrace reluctantly ended.

"Don't worry. I will." She followed him to the doorway, retrieved the paper from her porch step, and shut the door behind him. Forty minutes later, she'd eaten her breakfast, fed Frito, done her face and hair, and then changed for work. A quick check of her watch told her she had twenty minutes to wait. Just long enough to read the morning paper. She settled into her favorite corner of the couch and began unfolding the paper.

But Frito had other ideas. With a demanding whine, he pawed her leg, then trotted to the back door, a look in his eyes that bordered on desperation. Housebreaking the mutt had been a near impossibility. But she had to give him credit; once he caught on he refused to do his dirty deed in the house.

"Okay, I'm coming." She walked through the sunroom, decorated with plants and wicker furniture, to open the back door. Just as Frito ran to his task, her doorbell rang. Expecting Brad, Alissa hurriedly shut the back door and just as hurriedly clicked the lock into place.

CHAPTER 21

On the doorbell's third chime, she opened the door to see Mrs. Docker smiling her greeting. The elderly lady, her gray hair styled conservatively, peered at Alissa through thick glasses.

"I'm sorry to bother you so early. But I'm picking up a friend for breakfast in thirty minutes. I felt like you'd be leaving for work soon, so I thought I'd just drop by and tell you what I remembered about that note you found."

Alissa didn't say anything for several seconds. She couldn't. She was too busy studying Mrs. Docker's hair. *Think,* she commanded herself. Was Mrs. Docker's obvious wig the same color gray as what she'd glimpsed in her office last night?

The elderly lady, dressed in navy double knit, waited patiently for Alissa to invite her inside.

Surely a senior citizen in her eighties

wouldn't threaten someone's life. She lived in a retirement home because of her health, for Pete's sake. And all she wanted to do was tell Alissa what she'd remembered about the note. Maybe her story would explain Alissa's finding the name "Louanne" so familiar. Deciding Mrs. Docker was harmless, she opened the door wider. "Come in. Would you like some coffee?"

"No, no." She hobbled into the living room and seated herself on the couch. "Like I said, I can only stay a minute," she said in a high soprano voice that slightly shook with age.

Taking the chair opposite her, Alissa waited for Mrs. Docker to begin, and hoped she hadn't made yet another error in judgment as with Richard Calbert. Contrary to Alissa's original impression, he was apparently not trustworthy.

"I got to thinking after we talked, and it finally dawned on me about that note."

Alissa scooted to the edge of her seat.

"And?" she prompted.

"Well, shortly after I bought this house, Whit Jenkins told me about a terrible neighborhood scandal between the woman who owned the house before I did and Claire Allen's husband. His name was Richard, too, by the way."

"Oh?"

"Yes. It seems the woman who lived here before me — her name was Louanne Young — and Richard Allen were having an affair. Nobody knew anything about it until the two ran off together to Australia. Now here's the real twist. The plane they were on crashed over the ocean with no survivors. It was a terrible crash. Ten years ago, it was. I remember the media doing coverage on it for weeks." She patted the back of her gray wig. "Anyway, that's all I know. But I think that note you found was the very one that planned their rendezvous. Why I didn't see it for all those years, I'll never know."

Alissa's mind whirled with this news. "Well, it was actually stuck in the closet and rather hard to see." She stared at the phone as the reason for her familiarity with the name "Louanne" teased her mind.

"I never met Louanne, but Whit Jenkins said she was attractive. Blond hair, brown eyes, and thin-framed. I guess a whole lot like you. He said Claire was really devastated when she found out."

"Louanne had the same coloring? Are you sure?"

"That's the way Whit described her, 'course that's been ten years ago. I could have forgotten." Alissa's heart pounded in her throat as her mind finally focused on a recent memory. *You're in big trouble, Louanne.* The voice mail she'd received the day of her wreck! She'd shrugged it off as a wrong number, but maybe it wasn't. Maybe the person calling had intended the message for Alissa because she resembled Louanne, her husband's former lover. Claire Allen. Was she Alissa's adversary?

Her mind raced to the bones in Brad's backyard. Two bodies. Two people were supposed to be on a flight to Australia, a flight that crashed with no survivors. Had they ever boarded the plane? Or had someone murdered them before they had the chance? Was that someone Claire Allen?

"Dr. Carrington, are you all right?"

"Yes," she croaked, her cheeks as cold as a tombstone. "I — I — it's just that I think I need a drink of water." A drink of water and a tranquilizer. She had to call the police.

"Well, I won't keep you any longer. Like I said, I've got a breakfast engagement, and I know you have to get to work."

"Thanks for — for stopping by." As politely as she could, Alissa rushed Mrs. Docker out of the house. She then securely locked the front door and turned toward the telephone. But that was one phone call Alissa couldn't make. For standing behind the chair she'd just vacated was Claire Allen, holding an automatic revolver. Claire Allen, wearing an ill-fitting gray wig. Claire Allen, her lips stretched in smug victory, her eyes glazed in fury.

Alissa's heart raced in uncontrolled panic as cold sweat swept her body.

"Did you think you could escape, Louanne?" she sneered.

"How — how did you get in here?" Alissa croaked.

"You're just as stupid as you always were. Your back door was unlocked."

Frito. She'd let him out and thought she'd relocked the door. How could she have been so careless? Her lips trembling, Alissa inched toward the telephone.

"Stop!" Claire commanded, waving the gun for emphasis. "We're going to talk, and then you're going to die again."

"Again?"

"Don't play dumb with me, Louanne. You and I both know you escaped from your grave. You can call yourself Alissa Carrington all you want, but we both know you're Louanne Young come back to life."

"Those bones in Brad's backyard —"

"Of course. Don't you remember me making you and Richard march to Mr. Jenkins' newly tilled rose garden? It was so easy to

231

shoot you both, while you huddled together beside that fresh dirt like two love-crazed teenagers."

"You're — you're confused. I am not Louanne." Her mind spun. Was this what it felt like to face death? This sinking feeling of finality, of the past remembered, the future denied?

Claire tilted her head back and cackled hysterically. " 'I'm not Louanne,' " she mocked. " 'We're not having an affair! Oh please, please, please, Claire, don't kill me.' " She sobered, her eyes as piercing as a deranged demon's. "You were a liar then, and you're still a liar!"

Alissa stumbled backward.

"I said don't move!" Claire demanded. "I'm not through talking to you."

Alissa stopped, but her heart felt as if it were going to jump out of her body.

"Do you see this?" Claire fumbled in the pocket of her black knit pants to produce a tarnished gold watch, the same watch Alissa had given to Richard Calbert.

Alissa gasped. "Richard gave you the watch?"

"That idiot?" She cackled again. "No. I took it from his car. I was watching when you gave it to him. That Calbert man is so helpful in his stupidity. The very night I murdered you and my Richard in Jenkins' backyard, Calbert invited Whit Jenkins over for dinner. So with Whit gone, his new rose garden was free for me to bury you in. The next day, Whit planted his roses on your bodies and never even suspected." She looked down at the watch. "I also buried the watch because — because I couldn't bear to wear it. I knew I had to retrieve it when your bones were dug up, but I made the mistake of dropping it in your yard."

Alissa thought about the person running from Brad's house the day she'd met him. That too had been Claire Allen.

"Do you know how valuable this watch was to me? My Richard give it to me on our tenth anniversary." A sob, slow and wretched, broke her words. "Right before he met you."

"Mrs. Allen, I am not Louanne," Alissa insisted, her voice quaking. "If you'll just listen to me. You need help —"

"Shut up! I don't need help. I'm the one who was smart enough to pull off a murder, and no one suspected. Do you know what I did after I buried you and Richard?"

Alissa remained silent.

"Do you know?" Claire shrieked.

"N–no."

"Richard was a pilot. I used his password

to get into the airline's computers. Then I hacked into the boarding log for the flight and confirmed that Richard and you had boarded. That way, as far as the airline was concerned, Richard and you flew to Australia."

"Oh, really?" Alissa hoped her feigned interest would keep Claire talking.

"Yes. Pretty smart, huh? I was worried about Richard's and Louanne's families, though. I figured they would eventually wonder why those two lovebirds" — she said these last words with a twisted snarl on her face — "didn't write. Then the plane went down. Do you know how relieved I was?"

Alissa stared at her.

"Do you?"

"N–no."

"I was certain that fate had smiled on me. Then . . . then you escaped from your grave! Now it's time for you to die again. And this time, I'm going to fill you so full of bullets you won't ever escape your grave again."

"Please . . ." Alissa's eyes stung with tears, horror, of life denied. *Please, Lord, don't let her do it!*

An animal-like gurgling deep in her throat, Claire gripped the gun with both hands, pointed it at Alissa's forehead, and pulled the trigger.

Brad heard the muffled gunshot as he locked his front door. And the same instinctive fear that had gripped him yesterday gripped him today. Alissa. The shot sounded as if it came from her house.

His heart felt as if it sank to his feet as he raced toward Alissa's front door. Had that maniac somehow managed to enter her home in his absence? He lambasted himself for leaving her and at the same time prayed his assumptions were those of an overactive imagination.

After bounding up her porch stairs two at a time, Brad skidded into the massive wooden door and unsuccessfully tried the knob. It was locked. He pounded against the door with both fists. "Alissa?" he yelled.

No answer. His desperation rising to new heights, Brad rammed his shoulder against the door only to receive a ravaging pain up and down his arm.

"Alissa?"

Another gunshot, it sounded like the explosive claim of death itself. This time, Brad was certain the noise came from her house. He also knew he'd have to take a different route into the house. Glancing toward the window to his right, he sprang into action. One swift kick, and the glass shattered into a million fragments.

"Brad, no!" Alissa called, her voice full of surprise, fear, and something close to relief. "I — I've got the door."

"Alissa?" His heart stilled. "Are you all right?"

She flung open the door and stumbled into his arms. "Barely," she said, her voice breaking. Her lips quivering, she looked from Brad to the gun in her shaking right hand.

A moan, soft and pain-filled, floated from near the couch.

"Claire Allen," she said in answer to Brad's unasked question. "We need — we need to call the police and an ambulance."

"You shot her?" Brad croaked.

"Yes. But she almost shot me first." Alissa cringed. "If it hadn't been for Frito attacking her, I'd be dead." She spoke with as much calm as she could. "I'd put him out and — accidentally left the door unlocked. Claire must have left it ajar when she entered, and — and he followed her in, then attacked her from behind, just — just as she fired the gun." Another cringe. "Thank the Lord, Frito's impact knocked the gun from — from her hand, and the bullet missed me. I — I grabbed the gun and had to shoot . . .

236

in self-defense."

Brad stepped into the living room to see Claire writhing on the floor, clutching her right thigh, and Frito growling only inches from her. "She came after you even though you had the gun?"

Her face pale, Alissa nodded then mouthed, "She's crazy." Aloud she said, "Get a towel from the kitchen and see if you can slow her bleeding. I'll call the police."

That evening, Alissa sat in Brad's dining room, feeling like royalty as he served her his own special pot roast, baby carrots, and scalloped potatoes. "I had no idea you were such an excellent cook."

"There's a lot you don't know about me," he teased.

"I guess I'm on a course of discovery, then."

"We're both on a course of discovery." He reached across the table to squeeze her hand. "I'm just glad you're still alive to discover."

"Me, too." Alissa rolled her eyes. "If it hadn't been for Frito, I'd have a lot more than looks in common with Louanne Young. That dog was spoiled before, but as far as I'm concerned, now he can have anything his little heart desires." She sighed. "Poor Claire." Alissa reflected upon the pathetic insanity in the woman's eyes.

"Poor Claire? Poor Claire almost killed you. And she did kill her husband and his lover."

"I know. But it finally got to her. I don't think her conscience could let her get away with it. And when she saw me . . ."

"She became confused?" Brad, ignoring his meal, rose to circle the table and take Alissa's hand in his. "That seems to be the general trend around here, because the same thing happened to me. I haven't known which end was up since I first saw you."

Alissa stroked his hair. "The feeling's mutual," she muttered, her stomach fluttering with his closeness.

"You might as well be warned," he continued. "I plan to be a big part of your life from now on, probably forever."

"I don't expect anything less," she whispered against his lips.

ABOUT THE AUTHOR

Debra White Smith, author of the best-selling historical series, *Texas,* continues to impact and entertain readers with her life-changing books, including The Jane Austen Fiction Series, the Sister Suspense Series, *Romancing Your Husband, Romancing Your Wife,* and *It's a Jungle at Home.* She has been an award-winning author for years with such honors as Heartsong Presents Top-10 Reader Favorite, Gold Medallion finalist (*Romancing Your Husband*) and Retailer's Choice Award Finalist (*First Impressions* and *Reason and Romance*). Debra has about 50 book sales to her credit and, since 1997, has been blessed with over a million books in print. Her book, *The Neighbor,* which is a part of this collection, was the second book Debra published.

The founder of Real Life Ministries, Debra speaks at events across the nation and sings with her husband and children. She has been featured on a variety of media spots, including The 700 Club, At Home Live, Getting Together, Moody Broadcasting Network, Fox News, ABC Radio, Viewpoint, and America's Family Coaches. She holds an M.A. in English.

Debra lives in small-town America with her husband of 23 years, two children, and a herd of cats.

To write Debra or contact her for speaking engagements, check out her website:

www.debrawhitesmith.com
or send mail to
Real Life Ministries
Debra White Smith
P.O. Box 1482
Jacksonville, TX 75766